Praise for *Cross My Heart,*
THE HIDDEN DIARY, book 1

Cross My Heart was *very* descriptive (but not, like, overloaded!) and fun. It's a touching story that a lot of girls can relate to because of their own busy parents. I liked the mystery, too!

> Lilly, eleven years old, daughter of Liz Curtis Higgs,
> author of *Bad Girls of the Bible*

Mama mia! *Cross My Heart* was a great book! I liked the way the author left you hanging at the end of each chapter. It made you want to keep reading. I could really relate to some of the characters, and Claudette made me laugh. You'll love this book! Cross my heart!

> Tavia, ten years old, daughter of Deborah Raney,
> author of *A Vow to Cherish* and *Beneath a Southern Sky*

This book was really good, interesting, and fun. I couldn't say I had one favorite part because I loved the whole book! I couldn't put it down.

> Tyler, eleven years old, daughter of Lisa E. Samson,
> author of *The Church Ladies*

I couldn't put this book down! I guarantee you'll love *Cross My Heart,* and it will keep you on the edge of your seat.

> Marie, thirteen years old, daughter of Terri Blackstock,
> author of the NEWPOINTE 911 series

Cross My Heart is a very exciting book. Lucy . . . meets new friends and learns about God. I know my friends will love this book like I did. Maybe we'll find a hidden diary somewhere, too.

> Madelyn, nine years old, daughter of Cindy McCormick
> Martinusen, author of *Winter Passing*

I think Lucy and Serena are really cool. I can't wait to read the next HIDDEN DIARY book.

> Bethany, nine years old, daughter of Janet Holm McHenry,
> author of *PrayerWalk* & *Girlfriend Gatherings*

Books by
Sandra Byrd
FROM BETHANY HOUSE PUBLISHERS

THE
HIDDEN
DIARY

Change of Heart

SANDRA BYRD

BETHANYHOUSE

MINNEAPOLIS, MINNESOTA

Published by Bethany House Publishers
A Ministry of Bethany Fellowship International
11400 Hampshire Avenue South
Bloomington, Minnesota 55438
www.bethanyhouse.com

Printed in the United States of America by
Bethany Press International, Bloomington, Minnesota 55438

Library of Congress Cataloging-in-Publication Data

Byrd, Sandra.
    Change of heart / by Sandra Byrd.
        p.   cm. — (The hidden diary ; bk. 6)
Summary: Lucy and Serena are enjoying a week of swimming, kayaking, and the annual competition for the Golden Pig's Foot award, but Lucy faces a tough choice when she discovers a shocking secret about another camper.
    ISBN 0-7642-2485-9 (pbk.)
    [1. Christian life—Fiction. 2. Friendship—Fiction. 3. Camps—Fiction. 4. Secrets—Fiction. 5. Santa Catalina Island (Calif.)—Fiction.] I. Title.
    PZ7.B9898 Ch   2002
    [Fic]—dc21   2002002711

*To these wonderful girls
who faithfully read each manuscript,
making sure everything is just right.
Thanks for your hard work.*

*Amy Abelein
Jenny Hiestand
Lydia Hunt
Erica Torrey*

Contents

The Golden Pig's Foot

Saturday afternoon . . . . D Day minus six

Lucy waited at a glass table outside of Sweet Dreams, Avalon's ice-cream and candy parlor. Every minute or two she stood and looked up and down the street and then sat down again. Summer sunlight coated her from top to toe like a dipped cone.

Hidden diary time! Lucy waved as Serena walked around the corner.

"Ready for camp?" Serena pulled up a chair.

"I hope so."

Someone tapped Lucy on the shoulder. Lucy turned and smiled as Erica and Amy sat down in the chairs next to her and Serena.

Lucy locked eyes with Serena, but neither said anything right away. Lucy kept herself from looking toward Serena's worn bag, which held their hidden diary. The old diary was just for the two of them—no matter how great Amy and Erica were.

"We're on our way to get more sunscreen," Amy said. "My mom bought that purple spray stuff, and I don't want to smell like grape bubble gum at camp. What are you guys doing?"

"Talking about camp."

"It'll be great. I'm so glad you're coming with us this year," Erica said to Lucy. "We're all hoping and praying that we win the Golden Pig's Foot. This year is our very last chance to win one."

"Win the *what*?"

Serena, Amy, and Erica began to giggle. Erica explained. "Every year at camp they hand out an award—a Golden Pig's Foot. It's not a real pig's foot," she rushed on to explain. "It's just a joke since there are wild boars on the Island. It's like a trophy."

"Ah," Lucy said.

"The cabins compete," Amy said. "Girls against girls, boys against boys. Every day the whole camp does stuff that adds to the points. Like diving."

"I love diving," Lucy said. "I'm on the diving team at home."

"Great! There's other stuff, too. You get points for rope climbing or art or swimming relays, that kind of stuff."

"Bunny handling, archery," Erica chipped in. "And every year, the cabin who wins gets the trophies to take home—the Golden Pig's Foot. Ta-da!"

"This is our last year to get one," Serena said. "Next

year we'll all be thirteen and go to teen camp instead."

"Your brother got a Golden Pig's Foot a few years ago, didn't he?" Amy asked.

Serena nodded.

"Mine too. Our cabin always comes close, but we never quite win." Amy sighed. "So what's going to be any different this year?"

Lucy sipped her pop again and noticed, all of a sudden, that the table had gone quiet. She looked up to find all eyes on her.

"Well," Erica ventured, "Lucy's what's different this year."

Most of the other girls going to camp this week—in fact, most girls anywhere on Catalina Island—either lived there or came there every summer. Lucy's family, though, was just staying on Catalina, in the town of Avalon, for one summer. Lucy's dad researched plants for his job at the university.

"Jenny was sad she couldn't come this summer," Erica continued. "Last year was the first year she went. And Julie's even coming for the first time. You know how close they are. Anyway, if we do win a Golden Pig's Foot award, we could ask for an extra one and bring it home for Jenny! Think how glad she'll be that she gave Lucy her spot at camp this summer."

Lucy didn't feel warm and coated now. She felt hot and drippy. "Why will *my* being here make a difference?"

"Well, for one, you're athletic!" Serena said. "As much as we love Jenny, she's not into athletics. Most of the things we get points for are sporty things."

Yeah, I'm athletic, Lucy thought. *In softball. But I've never shot a bow and arrow in my life. Or climbed a rope.* She looked down at her sensitive, piano-playing fingers.

"And you are really good with animals," Amy chipped in. "Like when we all were taking care of the puppies."

Puppies, Lucy thought. *Not rabbits. What in the world is bunny handling?*

Amy reached over and squeezed Lucy's hand. "We're really glad you're coming this year. And you'll have fun, too."

Erica stood up. "It's our last year. If all of the rest of us can hold our own from last year, with the addition of our secret weapon"—she winked at Lucy—"we're sure to win. You won't let us down!"

Then Amy and Erica said good-bye and headed toward the pharmacy to buy their sunscreen.

"Ready to read the diary?" Serena asked. "We'd better get going. I still have to finish packing."

Lucy nodded. "Bring it on!"

At the beginning of the summer, the girls had found a diary that was written in 1932 by Serena's great-grandmother and her best friend, Mary. Each week Lucy and Serena read a section of the old diary and determined to do something just like the diary girls had done during the section they read. No matter what.

Serena drew the hidden diary out of her bag. "Oh no!"

"What?"

"I didn't bring my umbrella, since we're not going to the beach." They always read the diary under Serena's big yellow beach umbrella.

Lucy set her chin in her hand, thinking. She spied the small vase of fresh flowers sitting in the center of the glass table.

She pulled a yellow daisy out from the vase. She leaned next to Serena and put the flower over their heads. "There!"

Serena giggled and opened the diary. "All right, all right. Put it down now before Jake comes out of Sweet Dreams and thinks we're immature."

Lucy laughed and laid the yellow flower on the table. "Jake's not working today. He's at home getting ready for camp," she said.

"Already checked, eh?" Serena teased.

Lucy's face flushed. "No! I just went in to buy a Dr Pepper, that's all."

Serena smiled and opened the diary.

" 'Dearest Diary,' " Serena began to read her great-grandmother's blocky writing.

"A new beauty shop opened up in town, and lots of the girls have been going. Last week two of our friends got their hair bobbed—cut short. Of course, women have been doing that for years in big cities, but not in our little town. We think it looks dandy. We'd like to wear pants once or twice, too. It's kind of daring."

Serena handed the diary over to Lucy, who normally read Mary's swirling writing.

"We have decided it is time to be fashionable, time for a change. _Now._ Should we ask permission? My father thinks young ladies must have long hair, so if I ask before we do it, he will say no. Serena hasn't asked her father. And she may not. Check back at the end of the week. We might be new Avalon fashion plates."

Lucy handed the diary back to Serena.

"Or we could end up with trouble. Till then, Diary, ta-ta!

Faithful Friends,
Mary and Serena."

Serena closed the diary and handed it back to Lucy. "Well, wearing pants doesn't seem awfully daring to me."

"Or shorter hair. But we need to make a daring change, a fashion change, something everyone will notice. Just like the diary girls."

Lucy agreed. "Of course. We will make a change—dramatic change! We promised to do something just like them." She snapped her fingers. "I have it!"

"What?"

"Let's dye our hair."

"What? For good?"

"Not for good." Lucy changed her idea on the spot. "How about one of those ones that highlights it for the summer, you know?"

"Do you have much experience in this?"

Lucy shook her head. "We could figure it out, though."

"On our own?" Serena reached her hand up and felt her long dark hair. "I heard that stuff makes dark hair go purple." She nodded toward Lucy's wavy reddish-blond hair. "And you could end up looking like a stop sign."

"Got any other ideas?"

Serena shook her head. "We'll think about it, okay? We have till Friday."

A little jolt hit Lucy. "We'll be at camp Friday."

Serena's eyes opened wide. "Yep. So everyone will see this time. We won't be able to hide whatever we choose to do at camp."

Lucy nodded. "We have a few days to make a decision. Is there anything else about camp I should know?"

"Well," Serena said, "do you care where you sleep at camp?"

"Near you," Lucy said.

"Of course," Serena said. "I mean top bunk or bottom bunk."

"Well," Lucy started. She didn't want to be greedy if Serena liked the top bunk, but she *had* asked. "I've never slept on a top bunk, and I think it would be fun . . . if you don't mind."

"Top bunk for you, then," Serena said. "I'd better get home. You want to walk together?"

Lucy shook her head. "I've got . . . something to do. I'll see you in a couple of hours when we drive over."

"Okay."

After she made sure Serena had walked all the way up

the street, Lucy turned the other way and stepped into the pharmacy. She bought a tiny tube of toothpaste and some new breath freshener. Even though it was two dollars, she thought the fold-up toothbrush would be cool to bring, too. "I love little travel sizes." She tossed a tiny bottle of lotion into the basket, too.

Now for the real business. Lucy scanned the rows of hair color. "Aha!" She found something she thought would be okay for both of them—the box said it lightened any shade of hair. Honestly, she couldn't think of anything else for them to do for the Diary Deed. It was better to be prepared. Wasn't that a camp motto?

Guaranteed to produce summer-beautiful hair! the blue box promised.

Lucy grabbed one and stood in line, waiting to pay. On the counter were bins of pencils and packs of gum and a basket of rainbow-colored rabbit-foot key chains.

"I never saw a green rabbit, so how could there be green rabbit feet?"

As she handed her cash over, Lucy thought, *I never saw a golden pig, either. But everyone's counting on winning a Golden Pig's Foot this year.*

Lucy walked against the light wind the whole way home. She'd have to hurry if she wanted to get back in enough time to finish packing and look up some information on the Internet about archery and bunny handling.

No matter what, she wanted the other girls to be glad she was on their team.

Confusion

Saturday afternoon and early evening . . .

"I need help on the Internet!" Lucy shouted as she opened the front door. She stepped through the living room and into the corner where the small home office was. Her dad tapped at the computer with his headphones on.

She patted his shoulder and he faced her.

"Hi!" He slipped the headphones off. "Ready to go?"

"I need help on the Internet. Looking up extremely important things."

"Today?" he asked. "Hadn't you better finish packing?"

"Yes." Lucy shifted her feet. "But I need some information on bunny handling, archery, and rope climbing."

"Bunny handling?" Dad scratched through his trim beard. "Before camp?"

"Yes," Lucy said. As she was about to explain, her mother called from upstairs.

"Please come here and see what I have laid out for you

to take. If I have to wash or iron anything else, I need to know now."

Lucy sighed and rolled her eyes.

"Be nice," Dad warned. "Your mother had only one day's notice about camp. She's doing the best she can."

"I know," Lucy said.

"And when you're packed, come back and I'll help you look up bunny handling." Dad slipped his headphones back onto his head; Lucy caught the voices coming through the headphones.

She wrinkled her nose. *Opera.*

She ran up the stairs, kicking off her flower-power sandals as she did.

"In here!" Mom called from Lucy's room. "I got your jean shorts, your overall shorts, some khaki shorts, a big assortment of T-shirts . . . sweats. I put the Seattle Mariners shirt in there in case everyone wears something from where they're from."

"Oh. The girls in my cabin are all from Avalon," Lucy said. "I might want to have something with Catalina on it. You know, be part of the team."

"Okay." Mom took out a *Catalina Beach Bum* T-shirt and carefully folded it. "Will this work?"

Lucy kissed her mother's cheek. She walked over to her dresser and set down the paper bag with the toothbrush, toothpaste, lotion, and hair coloring in it. Lucy rolled the top of the bag extra tight. "I have a few things to pack," Lucy said. "Stuff like jewelry, books." She casually walked away from her dresser. "Hair care stuff."

"Okay. Don't forget to pack something a little dressy

for the assembly on Friday night. I'll be excited to see what you've accomplished this week." Mom stepped out of the room. "Your bathing suit is there and your goggles. Tennies and socks, two pairs of pajamas. I'll go and get you a towel. Be back in a few minutes."

Mom closed the door behind her, and Lucy began to stack the neat piles of clothes into her open suitcase. First the shorts, the shirts, and the socks. Then everything else her mom had laid out. Lucy snagged the Bible next to her bed and laid it on top. In went her wallet, with fifteen dollars and thirty-five cents and a folded snapshot of her new puppy, Venus.

Lucy tugged on her Wired for Christ necklace. She always wore it, keeping Him close to her heart. *What other jewelry, though?*

Not her precious opal ring. And she didn't want the mood ring to get wet. *Maybe just earrings.*

Toothpaste, check. Toothbrush, check. Oh no! She was out of shampoo.

"Mom! I need your shampoo!" She ran into the bathroom. "I'm out."

Her mother pursed her lips. "Bring it home. It cost me a pirate's ransom, and I can't buy any more till we're home. They don't sell it here. I have only two bottles to last the summer. I'll use the other bottle till you get back."

Lucy grabbed the silver shampoo bottle and packed it, too. Then, when almost everything was ready, she picked up Tender Teddy and looked at him.

Did anyone else bring stuffed animals to camp? It's not like she brought him when she stayed overnight for one night, but . . . this was almost a whole week.

On the other hand, she didn't want to look like a baby. She closed her eyes for a minute and then decided to zip him into the front compartment of the suitcase, where he'd remain hidden if need be.

Last, Lucy lifted the small paper bag from the pharmacy. She took the other stuff out and packed it in the center of the suitcase in plastic sandwich bags. She didn't take the hair dye out, though. She left it concealed in the bag. She slipped that bag next to Tender Teddy and zipped them both into the darkness.

As soon as the compartment was zipped closed, Lucy's mother appeared back in her room. "Here's the towel."

Lucy smoothed it over the contents of her suitcase and then zipped the main section shut. "I guess I'm ready. Should we go downstairs?"

"Not yet." Mom shook her head.

"We've already talked about the rules, Mom. I promise I'll follow them."

Her mother smiled. "I know you will. I don't want to talk with you about the rules. I have something else in mind." She stood up and took the little green bottle of nail polish from Lucy's dresser. "Remember how you painted my nails last week?"

"Of course!"

"Well, I thought if we each had a fresh coat, we could look at our hands if we get lonely for each other. It will make us seem close even if we're apart."

Lucy's eyes moistened. Homesick feelings crept through

her heart, and she hadn't even left home yet. "Great idea, Mom."

They painted each other's nails and chatted. When their nails were dry, Mom went downstairs to fix a light dinner before they would leave for camp.

Lucy brought her suitcase downstairs and then into her dad's home office. "Bunny handling!" she called out, hoping she could be heard over the *Marriage of Figaro* booming through her dad's headset. "Rope climbing!"

But Dad had already turned the music off. In his hand was a printed page with the words *Bunny Handling* across the top. What could it be? Juggling bunnies between campers? Taming them with a whip and a chair like the lions at the circus? Ha! Lucy scanned the top few lines.

> *The safest initial approach with rabbits is to begin by stroking the top of the head. Do not offer your hand for a bunny to sniff the way you would to a dog, because most seem to find this gesture offensive and may attack (lightning-fast lunge with a snort). Most bunnies do not like having the tips of their noses or chins touched. Their feet also tend to be ticklish.*

Lucy took a deep breath. *I wonder how many points they take off if the bunny attacks you.*

"I couldn't find anything on rope climbing," Dad said. "I figure you just scoot up the rope."

"Can you print something out about archery, too?" Lucy's voice was unusually small in an even smaller room.

"Sure." As her dad input the words, he asked, "What is this for?"

Lucy explained about the Golden Pig's Foot.

"Archery, eh?" he said. "You ever shoot a bow and arrow?"

"No." For once Lucy would have been glad for her dad to give her the drawn-out university professor's explanation of exactly how to do it.

Instead he said, "Neither have I."

Lucy snatched the pages on archery and bunny handling and slipped them in the front pocket of her suitcase.

After cheese sandwiches and milk, Lucy's dad turned out the house lights, and the three of them waited on the porch for Serena and her parents.

A few minutes later the Romeros' borrowed Suburban pulled up. Most people on Catalina Island only owned golf carts to get around in. Serena's dad had borrowed the big vehicle from a friend so they could take the girls to camp.

"Come on!" Serena jumped out and grabbed Lucy's suitcase so Lucy could get in with her pillow and brand-new sleeping bag. Together they tossed it all into the back with Serena's stuff, a big camp-gear stew. The dads sat up front, the moms sat in the middle, and the girls had their own private space in the back.

"Where's Roberto?" Lucy asked about Serena's brother.

"High school camp. He went this morning," Serena said. "My dad teases that he's a chauffeur today."

They headed out toward the interior, and Mr. Romero slipped a card into the gate that separated the interior of the island from the main town of Avalon. The gate swung open and then closed behind them.

"I'm so excited. Rachel will be our counselor, you

know," Serena said. "She was last year. And you guys are such good friends. It's like it was meant to be!"

Lucy smiled. It did seem like it was meant to be. "Serena? About that Golden Pig's Foot award . . ."

"You'll do great." Her friend squeezed her hand. "It's meant to be, too!"

I can dive, Lucy reminded herself. *I can dive really well, after all these years. I'll probably get a lot of points with that, and it can make up for a lot of the other stuff. Maybe softball will be one of the activities!*

"Look! There's the Double C Ranch," Serena's mother called out. "Let's wave!"

Lucy waved with the others and asked Serena, "Why am I waving?"

"My mom's friend owns the ranch. They have horses and stuff. My mom went riding there when she was a girl. Hey—it might have even been there since the diary girls were around. Anyway, her friend Carla lets poor kids come from the city to ride horses there. Kids that are too poor for a vacation."

Time clicked by like the white stripes on the road, and soon they arrived at camp.

Welcome to Camp! was emblazoned on a wood canoe turned sideways at the camp entrance. Lucy noticed that a boar—a wild pig—was etched into the canoe as a permanent design, too. He seemed to have all of his feet.

Serena's dad parked the Suburban, and they all got out. Lucy looked around her as the dads unloaded the back of the car. The water was bright blue. Somehow, even though it was the same blue water she'd been swimming in for over a month, it seemed different. Dreamier. Faraway. Nearby were fire pits dug out on the beach for hot dog roasts, volleyball nets stretched out like wide-open arms, and a huge swimming pool with a diving board and a slide.

A slow smile spread across her face. *Thank you, God. Summer camp at last.*

They walked up to the little log cabin that served as the main office. After standing in line for a few minutes, Serena checked in first. Then she and her parents walked to the cabin while Lucy checked in. "See you in a few minutes!" she said.

Lucy's dad took longer to check Lucy in, since they hadn't yet paid for the week. Finally the man handed Dad a slip of paper. He handed it to Lucy.

"Wren! That's the name of my cabin!"

They walked the short path, past the dining hall with its big bell and the pool and the art hut. The boys were all heading left, Lucy noticed. She and her parents followed a wooden sign pointing right. They came to a cluster of cabins—the girls' area. Lucy said, "Look! Wren!"

A small, neat cabin with white bandannas in the window was a step away. It was within tossing distance of three other cabins—where the other girls would stay, Lucy figured. Lucy pushed open the door, expecting to find Serena waiting for her. Maybe Amy and Erica had already arrived, too, or some of the others!

She stepped inside. "Serena?" No one answered. Amy wasn't in there, either, nor Erica, Julie, or anyone Lucy knew. Instead, she saw three girls she'd never seen before. Mom and Dad followed her in, silent.

"Hi!" one of the unknown girls said. "My name is Jessica."

"I'm Lucy." Her mouth was dry. Lucy scanned the name tags on the top and bottom bunks. One empty bunk and six other names. Lucy didn't recognize any of them. None of her friends were in this cabin!

"Here's your name, Luce," her mother said. A red-ribboned tag with *Lucy Larson* hung on a brass hook next to a lower bunk. Above that was a name tag that said *Shannon Hendricks*. Not Serena Romero.

Lucy drew near to her parents, a little dizzy, and whispered, "What is going on?"

A Wren

Saturday evening and night . . .

Lucy heaved her pillow, sleeping bag, and suitcase on the lower bunk next to her name tag. Jessica's dad came over and introduced himself to Lucy's dad.

"I guess our girls will be taking care of each other this week, eh?" he said.

Lucy's dad smiled, but Lucy could tell it was a forced one. "Yes."

The other girls seemed to be waiting for Lucy to join in with them setting stuff up. She was dazed and just didn't know what to do. She didn't want to seem snobby, but . . . she just didn't belong there.

A young woman stepped forward, and as she did, the others turned their attention back to their conversations.

"Hello! I'm Helen, your counselor." She held out her hand.

"Hi," Lucy answered. She wiped the sweat off of her

palm and shook Helen's hand, as did her mom and dad. Helen showed Lucy around the cabin. Helen seemed nice enough. But it wasn't the same as having Rachel as her counselor.

Dad slipped over next to Lucy. "Now that you've seen the cabin, what do you say we leave your stuff here and go for a little walk?"

Lucy nodded. When they stepped outside, Dad said, "Well, this is a surprise! Let's get back to the office and see *what* is going on!"

Lucy and Mom nodded their agreement, and they headed back to the log cabin office.

"I really want to be with my friends!" Lucy said. "They're counting on me, and I'm looking forward to being together!"

The three of them waited while six other campers checked in. Finally it was their turn. "Can I do the talking?" Lucy asked.

Her parents nodded their agreement.

"Excuse me, but I think maybe I was placed in the wrong cabin," Lucy began.

The assistant director raised his eyebrows. "Really?" He shuffled through the papers. "Your name is . . ."

"Lucy Larson."

He found her sheet and said, "Yes, Miss Larson. You were the last girl to register. Yesterday, correct?"

"Yes. But I took the place of my friend Jenny, I think. Anyway, I thought she was in the cabin with our other friends." Lucy gave him Serena's, Erica's, and Amy's names.

"Ah, the girls in the Squirrel cabin." The assistant

director smiled. "I understand. We had two last-minute cancellations late last night. Because you were the last person registered, you were the person who needed to be moved in order to even out the cabins a bit. Kind of like a filler. To keep things even for the staff, we try to keep the numbers nearly the same."

Great, I'm filler. Like that stuff they put in hot dogs.

"My daughter was excited to come here and do things with her friends," Dad said. "And now she won't be with them. Is that what you're telling us?"

Oh no. A scene was just over the next hill. Lucy smelled it coming. Dad's skin reddened beneath his beard.

"Lucy can do everything she wants with her friends," the assistant director said. "Sit with them at meals, hang out together. Activities. And when the director gets back on Monday, I will speak with him about moving her into the Squirrel cabin with the others. Till then, I'm sorry, but I just don't have the authority to do that."

Lucy spoke up. "It's okay, Dad. We'll figure it out. It's only till Monday." *I hope.*

Dad turned to her. "Are you sure? Because we can stay right here till it's figured out."

Lucy noticed the impatient campers and parents sweating behind her, carrying bundles that were starting to fall apart, checking their watches.

"It's okay. I'll call you on Monday if it doesn't work out."

Dad nodded his approval, and they stepped away from the counter and went to find the Squirrel cabin. It was right across from Wren.

When Lucy stepped inside the room and saw all of her friends unpacking, the full weight of her loss hit her.

"Where have you been?" Serena asked. "I've been worried!"

Lucy explained, and Amy and Erica hugged her.

"Don't worry. Mr. Rice, the director, is really nice. He'll fix it on Monday." Serena patted the top bunk. "This bunk will stay open just for you. We can sit together at every meal and hang out in between. Then on Monday night we'll have a big celebration. By then you'll be an official Squirrel!"

That is, if *I'm an official Squirrel.* Lucy knew Serena was thinking something similar, just by the shadow across her smile. Neither of them said it, though.

"If you look through the window by your bunk, you can see my bunk in Wren."

Serena peered through the dust-crusted window next to her bunk. "I see your stuff! So I'll be able to see you." She stopped. "Hey! It might be kind of cool if we could signal each other with our flashlights, you know?"

"What do you mean?"

"Tonight. Three flashes means 'Good night, Faithful Friend,' " Serena said. "Watch for my signal tonight, okay?"

Lucy warmed a little. "Okay!" Having their own signal was kind of cool. Just like at home, where they could see each other through their bedroom windows.

The parents soon left, and Helen knocked on the door. After saying hello to Rachel, she turned toward Lucy. "Maybe you'd better come back to Wren and unpack."

Lucy sighed. The assistant director must have told

Helen about Lucy's predicament.

"I'll do everything I can to make your stay here happy," Helen said as she and Lucy walked into Wren.

Jessica asked Lucy if she'd like to sit with her for breakfast the next day.

"I've already promised to sit next to my friend Serena," Lucy said. "But thanks for asking."

Jessica smiled and went back to unpacking. She was the only one without a bunkmate—there were seven girls in their cabin. The Squirrels had seven girls, too.

A new girl stood next to Lucy's bunk. That must be her bunkmate.

"Hi, I'm Lucy." Lucy held out her hand.

Shannon was twirling her hair between two fingers. "I'm Shannon." She let go of her hair long enough to shake Lucy's hand. Lucy stared for a minute at Shannon's long, shiny blond hair. Lucy's hair was a little . . . well, frizzy. She had curls that didn't curl neatly, but didn't flatten out too well, either. And it was not shiny, even with gel.

Shannon turned back to unpacking, and Lucy noticed Shannon had a lot of hair gear—clips and ribbons that matched every outfit, a silver-plated brush, hair spray. It took up a little more than half of the small dresser top that Lucy and Shannon were supposed to share. *Mama mia, it's* camp, *after all.*

Lucy turned her attention toward her own predicament. *Should I unpack my clothes?*

If she didn't take anything out of the suitcase, she'd be snubbing the girls in the room. It'd be like, *Man, I can't wait to escape you people!* It wasn't their fault, after all, that she didn't want to be here.

Jessica peeled a strip of licorice off of a stack of red. "Would you like one?" She held it toward Lucy.

Lucy smiled. "Sure." She sucked on the licorice rope while she unpacked her clothes into the drawer. Lucy left the paper sack from the pharmacy in the suitcase but took out Tender Teddy. As soon as she arranged him on her pillow, she saw Shannon look at her bunk.

Don't even think about making fun of my bear, Lucy thought.

Shannon took her eyes from Tender Teddy and went to her own suitcase. Lucy watched while Shannon unzipped it, took out a stuffed cat, and set it on her own pillow. Two smiles crossed the space between them.

Jessica squealed. "Hey! My mom tucked some notes into my suitcase!"

Lucy looked on with the other girls, giggling at the poetry. Then she looked down at her own green fingernails and giggled.

My mom sent me a love note in her own way.

"After church tomorrow morning, we'll go over the camp rules and activities and contests, okay?" Helen said. "But for now..." She strummed on a guitar, and they all sat in the middle of the room. Helen taught them some crazy camp songs. Lucy liked "Ham and Eggs" and "The Prune Song" best. They all laughed, and Helen ended the night, nearly whispering a soft song, "Angels Are Watching Over Me."

Lucy crawled into her bunk, stared at the stars out of

the cabin window, and remembered, *He never leaves us, even in a strange cabin with creepy noises outside.*

She snuggled her pillow and Tender Teddy and then reached for her Wired for Christ necklace, pulling it close to her heart.

Three flashes of light cut through the darkness. Lucy took her own flashlight and beamed it three times in Serena's direction. Warm sleep floated through the cool air, resting gently on Lucy.

She closed her eyes and let thoughts drift through her drowsy mind. Would she get to move over to the Squirrels on Monday, as Serena thought would happen? Lucy had her doubts. After all, the cabins would be really lopsided then for competitions and everything else.

Competitions! All of a sudden Lucy's eyes flew wide open in the dark. She sat straight up in her bed, nearly knocking her head on Shannon's bunk.

What if Lucy had to stay with the Wrens? She'd be competing *against* her friends for the Golden Pig's Foot! Maybe it wasn't such a bad thing that she'd never shot a bow and arrow or handled a bunny. Her bad scores wouldn't hurt the Squirrels and might actually help them.

But what about diving?

Divided

Sunday . . . D Day minus five

When Lucy opened her eyes the next morning, she couldn't remember for a moment where she was. After staring at the slivery wooden slats of the bunk above her head, she remembered. *Oh yeah, I'm a Wren.*

She slipped out of her bed and grabbed the plastic sandwich bag with her toothbrush and toothpaste in it. After slipping on some shorts and a T-shirt, she went over to the shared girls' bathroom.

"Lucy!" Amy was in the bathroom, too. "How are you?"

"Ah, fine," Lucy said. *Kind of.*

"I'll save you a space at the breakfast table," Amy said. "Serena probably already planned on it."

"If there's space," Julie chimed in. Julie was the one person in Catalina who did not like Lucy. She'd been rude to her since the day Lucy arrived at the island. Apparently,

Julie had arrived at the Squirrel cabin last night after Lucy had gone back to Wren.

Lucy turned her back to Julie. *No energy left over to deal with her today, too.*

Shannon was in the crowded bathroom already, almost done. Her hair was pulled back in little jeweled clips that matched her shirt and socks.

Lucy looked down at her own shorts and tried to smooth some deep wrinkles out. Even after she splashed some water on her hair, it wouldn't stay in place. She pulled it back into a ponytail instead.

"Good morning," Shannon said.

"Good morning," Lucy answered.

"Hello, beauty queens." Jessica strolled into the bathroom. Lucy broke into a grin and returned to her cabin to make her bunk before breakfast. Then she sped out before a Wren could ask her to sit with them for breakfast. She didn't want to hurt their feelings, but she wanted to sit with Serena.

Lucy stepped across the camp and into the dining hall. Helen called her over. "I've got a seat right here!" She patted the bench beside her. Shannon came into the hall right after Lucy and smiled at Helen as she headed toward her.

"Would it be okay if I sat with my friends in Squirrel?" Lucy asked, stopping some feet away from Helen's table.

"All right," Helen said. Lucy's heart sank even as she turned her back and headed toward the chow line. Helen's eyes had dimmed a little at Lucy's response. Lucy turned back toward Helen.

"I'll sit with you guys in church, though."

Helen smiled her pleasure and nodded her head.

Lucy dished scrambled eggs and a piece of bacon onto a scratched plastic tray and stuffed a napkin in her pocket. Then she found the Squirrels.

"I saved you a seat!" Serena said.

"Thanks." Lucy tightened her ponytail. As always, Serena's long dark hair was pulled back in a simple twist.

One of the counselors stood to pray, and then they all began to eat.

"I saw your flashlight signal last night," Lucy said with a smile. She poured a glass of juice for Serena. "Thanks!"

"I saw yours, too. But by tomorrow we won't need signals anymore. We'll be together!"

Lucy gave her a high five. "What's the competition today?"

"After breakfast is church, and then we can have a lazy day till the rope-climbing contest. Over a mud pond! Then tomorrow is Monday! Hooray!"

"I hope Monday is a hooray." Lucy still had her doubts. If she moved from Wren, there would be only six Wrens but eight in all of the other girl cabins.

"Can I have your attention, please?" A slight woman with a faint mustache called them over the speaker. "Welcome to camp! I'm Mrs. Rice. My husband, the camp director, will be back tomorrow. We hope this week will be memorable. Your counselors will go over the camp rules with you. They are there to help anytime. You can ask anyone any question. Please refrain from pestering the kitchen staff for snacks, though." She grinned.

A "boooo" roared from the boys' tables. Lucy kicked

Serena under the table, and Serena rolled her eyes.

"All activities this week are meant to bring you together as a team—each cabin as a team *and* all of us as the body of Christ. Just for fun, we are competing once again for the *very* valuable Golden Pig's Foot."

Some of the counselors giggled at the word *very*.

"Team standings are posted each night next to the dinner bell," Mrs. Rice went on. "They will be placed in point order at the end of each day—the top-scoring boys' cabin on top followed by the others, and the top-scoring girls' cabin on top followed by the others. All awards will be announced at the assembly on Friday night, even though you're *all* winners. Have fun!"

She sat down, and one by one the campers began clearing their trays, stacking silverware into dirty dish bins, and heading toward the chapel.

"We always sit in the back on the right," Serena said as they cleared their table.

"Oh. I, um . . . told Helen I'd sit with the Wrens," Lucy said. "Is that all right?"

Serena stepped back. "Well, of course it is. If that's what you want, it's okay with me."

Lucy squeezed her friend's hand. "We'll kayak together afterward, okay?"

"Okay."

Lucy went to the front left, where the other Wrens had taken up a row. There was a place next to Jessica, and Lucy headed toward it. As soon as she eased down the row, though, Shannon scooted over a seat. "Lucy!"

Lucy sat between Shannon and Jessica.

Helen stood up front for a while with the other counselors, playing her guitar while the worship began. Lucy closed her eyes, as always, and let the music sweep through her and take her far away and yet closer to God than almost anything else did. She felt Him there, right there in the Wren row.

I love you, Jesus.

One of the counselors gave a little talk.

"Is this a sermon?" Jessica whispered to Lucy.

Lucy, who had only been back to church for about a month, had no idea.

"I'm not sure it's called a sermon if a teenager gives it," Shannon teased.

Lucy giggled, but then listened to the counselor. He spoke about how he hadn't been a Christian, but when someone brought him to this camp just a few years ago, he watched how the other Christians treated one another. When his friend asked him if he'd like to yield his life to Christ, too, he'd answered yes!

It brought a tear to Lucy's eye. After all, her family had become Christians at camp, too—when she was a much younger girl. That was also when she'd received Tender Teddy.

I'm glad he's with me this time, too, she thought.

Afterward, when they all got ready to pray, Jessica reached a hand in Lucy's direction. Lucy was surprised but took Jessica's hand and in return held out a hand to Shannon. Shannon took Lucy's hand and held it lightly. She smiled at Lucy and at Jessica and bowed her head. Her jeweled clips were almost as shiny as her lovely blond hair, Lucy thought.

Maybe I should try a new gel. Or maybe . . . Lucy remembered the bag in her suitcase. A highlighter would give her hair a shiny look!

She glanced up and down her row—the Wrens all held hands now, as one team. All of their heads were bowed except Lucy's.

I'm sorry, God. I'm worried about my hair when everyone else is praying.

At the end of the service, Lucy said a polite good-bye and rushed off to kayak with Serena on that dreamy blue water during their free time.

🍄 🍄 🍄

After dinner that night came the first competition. Lucy's stomach felt as deep and murky as the pond beneath the rope.

"Ladies and gentlemen, boys and girls," Helen announced. "It's time to begin the nerve-racking rope climb!"

Lucy clumped together with the girls, both Wrens and Squirrels, and the other two cabins. The boys huddled on the other side of the pond.

"How does it work?" Lucy asked.

Helen explained, "You choose how many points you want to earn for the team. For one point, you climb up one knot on the rope and swing over the pond. For two points, you climb two knots high. And for three points, climb three knots high."

"What's the 'home run'?"

"To get a home run, you have to climb all the way up, hold on to the rope with no knots, and swing over the pond yelling like Tarzan!"

"Just don't drop into the mud," one girl laughed. "You lose points then and get awfully dirty!"

"I'm not dropping into a pond," Shannon said with real fear. Lucy couldn't puzzle out the look on Shannon's face.

Lucy watched as the other girls got ready to climb, rubbing a little dirt into their palms. She bent down, scooped some sand in her hand, and roughed them together.

Mama mia. What should I try to do? Lucy didn't know if she should try something really safe—like a single, which meant she wouldn't be getting too many points. That would be good for the Squirrels but bad for the Wrens. Which team was she trying to help?

"What are you going to try for?" she asked Serena.

"A double," Serena answered. "Look!"

Some of the boys they knew were going for the home runs. Jake and Philip did. A buzz-cut boy whooped like Tarzan as he swung back and forth over the pond. He slid down the rope, screaming, "Aaaahhhh," and plopped in.

"Oh man! The Monkeys lose a man! Monkey down!" teased one of the other boys' counselors in a loud voice. "Jungle disaster!"

"We're *still* the Hunky Monkeys," their counselor replied through a bullhorn. "And we will prevail!"

"Hunky Monkeys," Lucy said. "No way."

Serena giggled. "Jake and Philip's cabin is calling themselves the Winning Warthogs."

Serena climbed her rope to two notches—a double.

"Hey, Lucy, let's see how high you can go!" Jake called across the pond. Lucy had decided she'd just try to stay even with Serena, but now . . .

Lucy climbed past one knot, then another. It came easier than she'd feared. She held on at the second knot and glanced down. Serena waved. Lucy climbed up past the third knot, swung across the pond, and hollered, "Ahhhhhh!" like Tarzan. Once she was back on the ground, the Wrens cheered her and clapped her on the back. Serena grinned, but the other Squirrels were quiet and didn't look right at Lucy.

Were they mad at her? Should she try not to score points for the Wrens?

At the end of the day, when Lucy strolled past the boards with the team names painted on them, the Wrens were ahead. Four slats hung on each side of the dinner bell—boys on one side, girls on the other. The Monkeys' slat was at the top of the boys stack, with Warthogs on the hook just beneath, ahead of the other two boys' cabins.

On the girls' side, Wren hung on top, then Squirrel, followed by the other two girls' cabins. Lucy had a seasick feeling inside.

Later that night Lucy and most other Wrens went to shower up. After they had all come back and were in their pj's, Shannon went to the showers by herself.

Even from her bunk, head in a book, Lucy heard the whisper.

"She told Helen she had to shower by herself every night after everyone else was done."

"Why is that? Is she too good for us?"

It *was* strange. Shannon had done that last night, too, when nobody else had even showered.

The Director

Lucy waited till everyone else had gone to breakfast before she began her mystery mission. First, she dragged her suitcase out from the small storage closet in the back of the cabin. She left the front pocket zipped. Inside that pocket were two things: the packet of papers her dad had pulled from the Internet for her so she could help the Squirrels win, and the bag with the hair highlighter.

Tender Teddy would go in later.

Lucy put some of her clothes into the main pocket. That way, when it was time to move over to Squirrel, it wouldn't take so long later—or drag out the ordeal—in case the other Wrens were watching.

Lucy pulled her suitcase back to the storage closet and headed into breakfast in just enough time to grab a couple of pancakes and sausage.

The Wrens had finished eating and were leaving their

table. Lucy sighed and headed for the Squirrel table and sat next to Serena. There was no decision to make about where to sit.

"Today's the day." Serena squeezed Lucy's hand before getting up to empty her own breakfast tray. "Mr. Rice, the director, comes back."

"I'm praying that today is the day," Lucy said. She chewed a mouthful and thought for a minute before continuing. "I guess today's the day no matter what Mr. Rice says."

Lucy shoveled down her pancakes, wiped her hands on a paper napkin, and headed to the beach with Serena.

"We have kayaking and then lunch today," Serena said as they headed to beachcomb and kayak. "The water-balloon bombing contest is at two o'clock."

"Does it count for the Golden Pig's Foot?" Lucy asked.

Serena nodded. "Yep. So don't go stellar on everyone, okay?"

Lucy's hands clenched. Just one more competition against the Squirrels.

After lessons on the water with some other girls and a few counselors, the girls hauled their kayak up onto the beach. The girls devoured sandwiches and fruit and then went to the shuffleboard area for some friendly games. Afterward, they headed for the water balloon contest.

"Let's stop by the office and see if Mr. Rice is here," Serena suggested on the way over. Lucy looked at her watch. *Five minutes before two*. They still had time if they hurried.

The two of them ran into the office and found the

assistant director sitting there. Lucy's stomach hurt. He was nice enough, but what if Director Rice took the week off and never came back?

"We were wondering if, um, Director Rice is back yet," Serena started.

Lucy smiled. The normally shy Serena was speaking up on *her* behalf for once!

"No, young ladies, I'm sorry. But I do expect him back later today. Perhaps around dinnertime. And I'll be sure to let him know of your concerns."

Aha! So he would be back.

They raced to the balloon bomb. They had one minute to get there, and if they were late, their scores wouldn't count.

They arrived in the pit just in time. Shannon flashed a big smile of relief as she saw Lucy. Lucy smiled back.

I wouldn't let you down, she thought. *Oh. I'm thinking of the Wrens as my team.* Then, as she walked over to the Wrens, she thought, *Will I be letting them down if I leave the cabin?*

A big painted target stared from a concrete wall at the end of the shuffleboard area.

"There are five layers," a counselor explained. "If you hit the wall at all, it's worth one point. The closer you get to the center, the more points it's worth. If you hit the bull's-eye, you get five points, a major score. Okay?"

"Got it."

Even though the team boards never showed exact scores, Lucy couldn't help keeping track in her head.

The Squirrels went first. Four points, then ten, twelve,

Lucy counted. When the Squirrels had finished, Lucy counted a total of twenty-five points.

With the Wrens, Lucy also kept a silent score. Five points, seven, fourteen! When they finished, they were up to twenty-four. Lucy grabbed a balloon and readied herself to toss it. She pulled her arm back and got ready to toss it like a softball. It wasn't a softball, though, and it slipped. As she let go of it, the water balloon wobbled to the left and landed outside the bull's-eye. It barely hit the wall. One point.

Julie looked up at her and smiled. "Way to go," she said. "Thanks. You can help out in lots of ways besides diving." Lucy grew cold as she realized Julie thought she messed up on purpose to help the Squirrels. The Wrens looked away. Even Shannon said nothing; she just stood there, twirling her hair.

All of a sudden Lucy felt a whap on the back. A wet sting spread across her back and drenched her T-shirt.

A water balloon! Lucy turned and saw the group of Hunky Monkeys giggling.

"You are animals, you monkeys!" Jessica picked up a water balloon and lobbed it toward them. It hit the pack leader square in the chest. Before anyone could stop them, the girls picked up their balloons and pitched them in the direction of any boy around. They gave as good as they got. Lucy laughed harder than she had all summer.

Sometimes even boys could be fun!

A minute or two later, Mrs. Rice blew the whistle. "All right," she said. "Better go back to the cabins for quiet time." She checked her list. "Wrens and Squirrels, you're on KP tonight! Please report to the kitchen at four o'clock."

The girls hurried back to their cabins. Before they parted ways, Lucy asked Serena, "What's KP?"

"Kitchen Patrol. Two cabins take over dinner each night. I guess we'll be together sooner than we thought!"

Back in their cabin, the Wrens changed into dry clothes, Lucy hanging her wet ones on the edge of her bunk. After a little nap, she and the rest of the Wrens drifted out of the cabin and toddled single file to the kitchen.

When they arrived, Julie already had on a tie-dyed apron and was giving orders. Lucy rolled her eyes, but Serena just looked away.

Sometimes it bugged Lucy that Serena always stuck up for Julie.

"Lucy, you, Serena, and a couple of Wrens get to be the clean-up patrol," Julie ordered.

Lucy was about to comment when Serena whispered, "Let's just do it. Wendy will be there."

Lucy stopped. "Who's Wendy?"

"You'll see," Serena promised. "And it will give us time to check and see if Mr. Rice is here before dinner."

After helping prepare the food, Lucy tugged Serena's arm. "Let's go!" They strolled casually by the office. Lucy pretended not to look in the window to see who was behind the desk. "La la la, just taking a walk, not anywhere in particular, like past the office," she sang quietly. Serena laughed.

"Not yet!" the assistant director called out through the screened window as they passed by.

"How embarrassing! He saw us!" They took off running.

When they got to the dining hall, Serena pointed at the boards. "Look!"

The Squirrels were on top. Lucy gave a weak thumbs-up.

Tonight was Spinner Dinner, Serena informed Lucy.

"What's that?" Lucy asked.

"Everyone has to spin a big wheel to see what food they eat first."

Inside the dining hall, Julie, as head waitress, was manning the spinner. Serena laughed when Rachel got breadsticks, but the person behind her got a gooey piece of chocolate cake with vanilla ice cream to start with. Amy spun and got salad dressing and had to wait a full two spins before getting the salad, too.

Lucy started with fried chicken and came back to spin for dessert, and finally, a salad.

When she finished, Lucy followed Serena into the kitchen. "Cleaning up doesn't seem bad when it follows a cool dinner like that," Lucy said. She began to scrub pans. Jessica and Shannon were already there, and Jessica turned on the music.

"Gross!" Serena called from the sink. She was busily stuffing chicken skins into the garbage disposal.

"What?" The other girls ran over to see what she was pointing at.

"Hairs. Growing out of their dead skin."

"Ew." Lucy looked at the chicken skin. "Chickens have goose bumps. Isn't that funny?" She pointed to the lumps from which the hairs sprouted. "Do we get points for gross-est job?"

Serena wrinkled her nose. "No, but this is the last job and then we're done, I think." A moment later Serena's disgust turned to joy. "There's Wendy!" She ran over and hugged the young lady coming into the kitchen. Lucy thought she looked about twenty years old. And very cool.

"How are you?" Wendy asked.

"Great. This is Shannon and Jessica," Serena introduced them. "And my best friend, Lucy."

"Ah, Lucy," Wendy said. "My sister has told me a lot about you."

Lucy looked at her. Wendy looked familiar somehow. Had they met before? "Rachel!" Lucy finally burst out.

"Yes," Wendy said. "Rachel's my sister. I'm the kitchen manager, so I haven't met you yet. I hear that you're going to my dad's church in Avalon."

"Yes." Lucy smiled. The four girls sat down on the bench.

"Will you braid my hair?" Serena asked. She turned to the others. "Wendy went to beauty school. She's going to get married at the end of the summer, when her fiancé gets back from the Navy. Then she'll work at a salon wherever they move."

Wendy leaned over and braided Serena's hair. "Want me to do yours?" she asked Lucy. Lucy nodded, and Wendy braided her hair.

"Mine's too short to braid," Jessica said.

"How about you?" Wendy asked Shannon, reaching out to touch Shannon's hair.

"No!" Shannon backed off. "Don't touch my hair!"

"Sorry!"

Lucy felt bad for Wendy, who was only trying to help. *Man alive. Shannon doesn't have to be so rude.*

At that moment Wendy turned and greeted the man entering the room. "Hello, Mr. Rice."

Mr. Rice is here!

"Hi, Wendy. Do I have to spin for a meal?"

"No." Wendy smiled. "I'll get you some leftovers." As she prepared a plate, Shannon and Jessica said good-bye and headed back to Wren.

Lucy's heart beat two times fast and then once.

"Lucy Larson, right?"

"Right," she answered.

"We have a problem, Lucy. Maybe you can help me out."

Her heart sank. She'd be a nice kid and not make a scene.

"I brought two new girls with me tonight. Their parents are staying with friends on Catalina, and they wanted to come to camp. The only thing is, they want to stay together. Would you be willing to move to the Squirrel cabin so I can put them into Wren?"

Lucy leaped up. "Would I! Thanks!"

Serena jumped up, too. "Come on! Let's get you moved over!"

Lucy and Serena ran back toward the cabins.

"I think I'd better pack alone," Lucy said. "I'm not sure what they'll think."

"Okay. See you soon." Serena turned into Squirrel.

Lucy took a deep breath and walked into Wren.

Lucy heard strange voices inside the cabin. The new girls were there already. Her cabinmates would know she was leaving.

The Wrens were all there with the two new girls, who had piled their stuff on the one vacant bunk. Waiting for Lucy to leave, she supposed, so they could have hers, too.

She wanted to go to Squirrel, right? So why did it feel like she was letting someone down?

"I guess you guys know they're moving me back with my friends," Lucy said. "My other friends, I mean."

Everyone nodded.

"I understand. I'm glad we got to know you," Jessica said. "And we can still see each other, of course."

But it wouldn't be the same, like they were on the same team, anymore. And they all knew it.

Shannon slowly unhooked Lucy's name tag from the bunk and silently handed it to her.

Lucy packed the rest of her things and said good-night. Then she lugged her suitcase out of the cabin and toward Squirrel and all of her friends from Avalon.

"It's what I wanted," she whispered to herself. "Now I'm a Squirrel. I can help my friends win—go all out and try my hardest." Nothing could stop her from helping the Squirrels win now.

Could it?

A Squirrel

"What are you looking at?" Serena climbed up on Lucy's bunk after breakfast the next morning.

Lucy closed her Bible and pointed out the window. Thin yellow sunlight coursed through the trees, bumped off of the slate mountain walls surrounding the camp, and spilled onto the ground. "Isn't it beautiful? The view is much better from here than it was from Wren."

"Maybe it's because of what's *inside* the cabin and not outside," Serena said.

"My first day as a Squirrel." Lucy sighed with pleasure. "Thanks for saving the upper bunk for me. I know it seems like a little thing, but it means a lot to me." She pointed through the screen to the outside window ledge at a shed cocoon.

"Whatcha find?"

"A cocoon. Isn't it weird? A sluggy bug lived in there,

and then it broke out and was something totally new, a butterfly. It changed completely from the inside out."

Serena touched the cocoon. "One week in Sunday school, Mrs. Hicks said that's what we're like. God changes us into a completely new person from the inside out."

"We think a lot alike," Lucy said, smiling at her best friend.

"You know why I want to win the Golden Pig's Foot?" Serena asked.

"Because it's your last year to get one."

"Well, that. But also, each one of us will have one of them to take with us at the end of the summer. Some of us live on the Island all year, and some of us live in other places." She looked at Lucy. "You have to go back to Seattle."

"Shhh!" Lucy said. "Don't spoil it. We don't have to talk about that now."

"But what I mean is, won't it be great if we can each take back a trophy, something we know the other girls are looking at, too, no matter where they are? It will be a memory of our team, a keepsake of our friendships, all of us."

Lucy nodded, not wanting to think about leaving Catalina and going back to Seattle at the end of summer. How would her friends remember her? If they won, a lifelong keepsake would help. And she could dive well and help with that. The Golden Pig's Foot would be a forever memory of them working together as a team when they weren't a team any longer.

Also, Lucy remembered it was a new day. And only

three more days till the Diary Deed. They needed to make a decision. Today.

"Come on, guys," Amy called up to them. "Bunny handling in just a few minutes! Girls go first today."

Bunny handling. Lucy gulped. It was her first real chance to make some points for the team. *But some bunnies bite!*

First Serena, then Lucy climbed down from her bunk. On her way down, she pressed her palm against the name tag that said *Lucy Larson*, and then against the one right below it that said *Serena Romero*.

After pulling some shorts and shirts over their bathing suits, the Squirrels walked together to the bunny hutches at the back, shady area of the camp. The air was perfumed with the pine chips that lined their cages; it smelled like Christmas in July. The other three girls' cabins were already there. In fact, one cabin was already handling bunnies. Some looked like chubby calico kittens, breaking out in black spots. Some looked like midnight.

"Is this worth a lot of points?" Lucy could barely wait till the others were gone before she bombarded Rachel with questions.

"Kind of. Diving and archery are worth the most, because with diving you can aim for rings in the center of the bottom of the pool. Also, it depends on how good of a diver you are, how long you can hold your breath and see underwater. Lots of skills. Archery is the last thing, so it's worth a lot of points."

"What do we get judged on here?" Lucy whispered.

"The idea is to see how well you work with the

rabbits." Rachel sat next to her on a log. "It's an opportunity to be gentle and patient and to show how you react with animals. Don't worry, Lucy, you'll do just fine. It's all friendly competition."

Late last night Lucy had studied her paper on bunny handling again. "I, uh, heard that they could bite."

Rachel laughed. "Unless you pull on their ears or throw them against the ground, these bunnies won't bite you. They're used to kids. Just watch the others, relax, and do things slowly. Let the bunny get used to you. Offer it a treat. Wait for it to come to you."

Lucy let out her breath. No raging rabbit wounds in her future. "Why is that girl wrapping her bunny in a towel?"

"To keep its feet from kicking and to get a better grip. You get fewer points from it, but it keeps the bunny controlled."

"Oh no!" Serena said. Lucy turned to see one of the rabbits leap to the ground.

"Get it!" a girl from another cabin screamed as the bunny hopped madly about on the ground.

The boys had begun to gather for their turn with the rabbits just as this one escaped. "Hey—catch him before the chef does!" one of the boys called.

"That's the idea!" one of the other boys said. "Boys are in charge of dinner tonight. Rabbit stew for everyone!"

"Gross!" Lucy said, and the other Squirrels nodded their agreement. Finally one of the counselors threw a towel over the bunny and scooped it up.

Lucy couldn't help giggling at the wriggling towel. The

counselor returned the rabbit to a hutch to recover and got a replacement rabbit out.

"Points? Zero," Julie whispered.

Lucy wasn't saying anything. She'd never held a rabbit before, either.

The Squirrels stepped up next. Because Lucy was the last one into the cabin, she was number eight when their team competed, so she went last. Serena switched places with someone else so she could be number seven, next to Lucy.

Amy went first. She gently put her head near a blizzard of a bunny and made soft cooing noises. Amy moved her hand forward slowly, just a bit, with a tutti-frutti rabbit treat in her hand. The bunny wrinkled its nose and stepped forward. Amy reached forward, fed it the treat, and petted over its eyes. She picked the bunny up under the chest, scooped it under its backside, and walked around with it. Lucy watched, amazed, as the rabbit snuggled into Amy's chest. By the time she set it down, the judges were smiling.

"Great job!" Lucy whispered to Amy when she returned to the group. Soon it was Lucy's turn. Serena was beside her; she stepped forward and took a bunny the color of a rusty nail. Lucy walked up to a cage that said *Davy* and decided, *I'm not going to use a towel. I'll get more points for the Squirrels.*

She took a treat between her fingers and held it out to the bunny. "Here, bunny bunny," she cooed. "Davy is a good name for you. Your fur looks like a coonskin cap."

The bunny sniffed toward the treat and came close to Lucy.

Okay, just remember what Amy did. Lucy stroked Davy's head and then reached under his chest. She could feel his little heart beat and his chest suck air and then let it out. At that minute Davy began kicking his back feet. He wriggled loose in Lucy's hands.

Please don't freak out! Lucy wasn't sure if she was talking to herself or Davy. *And don't drop.* She looked over toward Amy, who made a scooping motion with her hand.

Yes. Lucy scooped up behind the bunny's rear quarters. Lucy looked back at Amy, who drew her arms into her chest. Lucy nodded and drew the bunny near her chest. Thankfully, the bunny snuggled in. She petted his back, his fur as soft as winter slippers.

After walking him by the judges, she set him down again and went back to the Squirrels.

"You did just fine," Amy said.

"Thanks for rescuing me." Lucy hung her head. "They'll probably take points off for that, won't they?"

"You'll get points for recovery," Amy said. "And besides, we're a team. I do some things well, and so will you, like diving."

Lucy saw that Jessica and Shannon were up next. Jessica had some trouble, just a little. As far as Lucy could tell, Jessica probably scored much like Lucy did—in the middle.

Just like Amy, though, Shannon handled the bunny perfectly. When she went back to the Wrens, Lucy called over, "Great job."

Shannon hadn't smiled when Lucy left Wren last night. She smiled now, though.

Once again, the Wrens and the Squirrels seemed to be

equal, though the other two girls' cabins had more trouble at almost every event.

Afterward, Lucy, Serena, and some others strolled to the pool. The boys were having a full-on belly-flop festival for fun.

Julie took off her cover-up and sat in the sun. She turned to Lucy and asked, "Why did you tell that snobby blond girl 'good job'?"

"I was just being nice," Lucy said. She wanted to add, "Something you might try sometime."

But that wouldn't honor anyone.

"Just remember whose team you're on now." Julie lay back on a pool chair.

"Wanna flop?" Lucy grinned at Serena, glad that the competitions were over for now.

"I will if you will!" Serena and Lucy headed over toward the board and lined up.

When it was Lucy's turn, she slowly stepped out onto the board. One foot in front of the other. She stood at the edge. The board was still; her diving coach taught them to never bounce till it was time to lift off, and then only one bounce.

Both boys and girls sat on the metal bleachers on each side of the pool, watching her. Jake and Philip and the rest of the Winning Warthogs called out to Lucy and Serena. Lucy smiled. The scratchy board beneath her feet felt pleasingly familiar, like a giant fingernail file.

In just a few more days I'll be back up here, doing a real dive for the Squirrels.

This time, though, Lucy reached up and out, forcing

her body to be as flat as the board she'd just launched from. After soaring through the air for just a few seconds, *splat!* She hit the water like a flipped pancake on a griddle. Her arms, legs, chest, and stomach stung, but it was worth it. When she reached the top of the pool and caught her breath, she got an earful of strong applause and whistles.

I'll be paying for that with sore skin. But she smiled when she swam to the side.

"Do you want to swim for a while or go play shuffleboard?" Serena asked.

Lucy wrung out her hair with a pool towel and looked at her red legs. "I think I'll stay out of the water for a while."

They went back to the cabin and changed into some dry clothes.

As Lucy opened her drawer, she saw the bag with the hair coloring in it. "I had a great idea last night when I was unpacking my stuff." She took the blue box out of the drawer and shook it at Serena.

"What is *that*?"

"Hair coloring." Lucy saw Serena's panic. "Temporary. You know, that sun stuff for the summer."

"When did you get it?"

"Before we left home. For the Diary Deed. Anyway," Lucy rushed on, "I had a great idea. Since Wendy is a hair stylist, couldn't she help us with this? At least she knows what she's doing."

Serena sighed. "Every time you tell me you have a great idea, I know it means I should put my seat belt on!"

"We don't have to use it if you don't want to," Lucy

promised. "But then we have to think of another Diary Deed. In three days."

Serena considered it before answering, twirling her nearly black hair around one finger. She stopped and faced Lucy.

"If we can't think of anything else, we'll dye our hair Friday afternoon. No matter what it's going to look like."

Shocked!

Wednesday . . . D Day minus two

Lucy awoke and realized it was still dark out. Who was shaking her?

"Shh." Serena took her hand from Lucy's shoulder and motioned for Lucy to come down from her bunk.

"What's going on?" Lucy asked. Serena shook her head and mouthed, "I'll tell you later."

Then she stepped down the ladder and Lucy followed her. She quietly slipped on a pair of sweats. Most of the other Squirrels were out shivering in the morning dew.

As soon as they had stepped away from the cabin, Serena spoke up. "We always serve breakfast in bed to Rachel one of the days we're at camp. We decided this week it was going to be Wednesday. I'm sorry I forgot to tell you—we decided when you were still a Wren."

Lucy yawned. "It's okay. Anything else I should know about?"

Erica spoke up. "Uh-huh! Tonight is the unofficial prank night at camp. We have to think of a prank to do tonight—and not get caught!"

A prank. Now, that sounded fun! Especially the part about not getting caught . . .

As they walked past the boards, Lucy noticed that the Squirrel board had dropped a notch. The Wrens were in first place!

"Uh-oh." She pointed it out to Serena.

"I noticed," Serena said. The other Squirrels looked glum, too.

"Don't worry. We've got lots of things left to do," Lucy said. "We can pull ahead. And I know we must be really close."

Even Julie smiled. "Diving is coming up."

The girls tumbled into the kitchen, still rubbing crackled sleepers from their eyes. The kitchen staff was already there.

"Aha, I see you've decided to get breakfast in bed for Rachel again this year," Wendy said.

"Yep. What can we bring her?" Julie checked her watch. "She's going to want to do demonstrations with us in a little while."

"Demonstrations?" Lucy whispered to Serena.

"She means devotions," Serena said. "I don't think she knows what that word means."

A few minutes later Wendy came out of the kitchen carrying a small Thermos of coffee, a plastic tray with bacon and scrambled eggs, and two slices of toast. She had wrapped plastic wrap around the whole thing. "To keep the bugs—or little Squirrels—away from the food." She winked at them.

Julie took the tray and Serena took the coffee. Lucy took the back of the line, trying to keep up with the others. *I am definitely a night person,* she thought.

When they got into the cabin, Lucy thought Rachel had shifted positions since they left, but the girls yelled, "Surprise!"

Rachel turned over and seemed surprised. "Well, I didn't expect a treat again this year!" she said. She sat up in her bed, the only one that was not a bunk, and Julie placed the tray on her lap. The girls all sat at her feet and talked with her while she ate.

After Rachel set the tray aside, she read out of a devotion book, and then they talked about it for a while. Lucy thought it was cool that the story was from Matthew, where she was reading, too.

"Ready for breakfast?" Rachel asked.

"Yes!" Each bright-eyed Squirrel scampered into the bathroom to get ready as quickly as possible. Most of the other girls were already gone. Lucy saw Shannon and Jessica and one other girl leave. They waved to her, and Lucy called back, "Hi."

I wonder who is on the bottom bunk beneath Shannon now?

She didn't wonder too long. She had other things to think about—the swimming competition, tonight's hot dog roast—hosted by the boys—and the prank, of course.

"Let's swim!" Lucy climbed into the pool after Serena.

"This way we'll get used to the water before the competition."

"Okay, everyone, attention!" one of the boys' counselors called through the bullhorn while Helen held up two kickboards.

"What do these look like to you?" Helen asked.

"Kickboards!" one of the boys called back.

"Two points off for the Warthogs for being a smart aleck."

When the boy began to protest, the counselor said, "Just kidding."

"The Ten Commandments!" one of the new Wrens called out.

"Right!"

"Those new Wrens are smart *and* athletic," Serena whispered to Lucy.

Lucy nodded. The boards did look like the Ten Commandment stones when they were turned with the curvy part on top.

"We're going to make the ten commandments of camp." Helen pulled out a black marker and waited for people in the huge pool and alongside to call things out.

"Boys always eat first!" one of the guys yelled.

"Sounds good," the teenaged counselor nodded his head.

Helen shook her head, and the boys booed.

After a while they did mark out ten commandments, including showing up for chapel, being thankful, and having fun. Lucy thought about working with all of her new friends and called out, "Teamwork!"

Several people yelled their agreement, and "teamwork" was added. Lucy blushed through her already sun-pinkened skin.

"Cool, your first year at camp and you added a commandment!" Serena ribbed her. Lucy elbowed her back.

The counselor called through his bullhorn, "Let the swim competition begin!"

This time the boys went first. Lucy cheered for Jake. She cheered for Philip, Jake and Serena's friend, too.

When it was the girls' turn, Lucy swam her hardest and looked at the time at the end. They got points for both technique and time. Lucy looked over the other girls swimming. She whispered to Serena, "The other two cabins are . . . well, I don't mean to be mean, but . . ."

"Not too much competition," Serena finished.

"Right. I think we're about even with the Wrens."

Later that afternoon, the girls went back to the cabin and changed clothes and prepared for their quiet time.

"Could Lucy and I have our quiet time by the beach?" Serena asked Rachel. "We'll be praying. I just thought it might be cool."

Rachel nodded her agreement.

The girls snuck out to the water. Once outside, Lucy and Serena walked along the surf first. "Sand fly," Lucy said, tweezering it between her first and second fingers. She dropped it and picked up a little crab instead.

"Crabs look like bugs." Lucy stared at its crooked pink legs and imagined them in hot water. She plugged her nose. Even small crabs smell like rotting garbage. "I'll think about this next time I dip one in butter."

They sat down on a skinned log and looked out onto the water in silence. Lucy reached into her pocket and pulled out her plastic Jelly Belly case. "Want one?"

Serena laughed. "I wondered if you'd brought that! Of course I want one." She chose Wild Blackberry; Lucy took some Dr Pepper beans.

"The only Dr Pepper I'll get all week, I guess." She giggled.

After they finished chewing, the two of them bowed their heads in prayer. Lucy, copying Jessica's action in church the other morning, reached over and held Serena's hand while they prayed.

Lucy prayed for the others in their cabin. And Shannon.

Afterward, they had a few more jelly beans.

"Serena?"

"Yeah?"

"Are the girls in our cabin, all the Squirrels . . . are they all Christians?"

Serena shook her head. "I don't think so."

"Why did they come to a Christian camp, then?"

"They wanted to come with us, I guess," Serena said.

"I know Erica is a Christian. I was just thinking about what you'd said about Julie not knowing what devotions are. I . . . I didn't really use that word myself before."

Serena nodded. "I understand. I don't know about Amy or Betsy or Kelly. Or Julie."

I doubt Julie is. Lucy felt ashamed as soon as she thought that. You couldn't always judge the inside by the outside. Especially when you didn't know a person very well.

"Do you think Shannon is one?" Serena asked. Lucy looked up at Serena. For the first time since they'd been friends, Serena looked a little . . . jealous.

"I think so," Lucy answered. "By the way she talked and prayed and stuff in church." She reached over and reassuringly squeezed her friend's hand.

The surf rolled in, and a few minutes later the girls went into dinner.

After dinner they all went to shower. No one was in there but the Squirrels this time. Maybe the other girls had already showered and were planning their pranks.

Lucy toted in her soap, her new toothpaste and brush, and her mother's expensive shampoo. *I hope no one asks to borrow any. Mom might freak if it's almost all gone.*

Afterward they all changed into their pj's and went back to plan.

It was prank time.

Rachel left them to plan, sitting on her bed in the corner, reading.

"How about we throw handfuls of candy into each of the cabins and then run away?" Amy said.

"Well, who has candy?" Erica asked. "And they'd catch us before we could do them all."

"Not if we split up."

"Hmm." They sat in silence again.

"Remember last year when someone strung a 'personal item' up on the flagpole?"

"Yeah, that was kind of funny," Erica said.

"Well, who's going to donate the 'personal item?'" Lucy said. "I sure don't want anything of mine flapping around up there."

"Nothing embarrassing, girls," Rachel said without looking up from her book.

"We could put something else up there," Amy said. "Like . . . a flag! One we could make."

Serena scratched her fingernail against the floor. "What kind of flag? Made out of what?"

"Out of a T-shirt! With markers!" Lucy suggested.

"Let's put *Squirrels Rule* on it," Julie suggested.

Serena shook her head. "How about just *Girls Rule*. That way we can include everyone."

"Except the boys, of course."

"I don't know. I think the Monkeys are sort of nice," Amy said.

"Gross!"

They all agreed on the T-shirt.

Amy had a white T-shirt and Rachel had a marker. They wrote *Girls Rule* on the shirt, and after it was good and dark and the only sounds were the rustling of the trees, the girls slipped out into the night.

Julie grabbed the flag hook, and Amy handed her the T-shirt. They hooked it on in such a way so that the T-shirt stayed completely open. Serena ran the flag up the pole, and they all snuck back to their cabin.

Just as they arrived and the others went in, Lucy glanced back at the bathroom and said, "Oh no!"

"What?" Serena said.

"I've got to go in the showers to get my mom's expensive shampoo. I'll be right back."

Serena nodded and went into the cabin. Lucy snuck back to the bathroom. She'd left the shampoo in the shower stall. Her mom would kill her if it wasn't there.

Lucy saw the back of the director's wife in the bathroom stall area. *She must be cleaning up.* When Lucy entered the shower area, she could hear that water was running.

Who would be taking a shower at this time of night?

She walked closer, trying to remember which one she had been in. As Lucy approached a curtained stall, she saw something strange.

What was hooked on the wall of the shower stall? It looked like someone's hair. Goose bumps rippled up her neck. It looked like hair she recognized. Shiny hair. Blond hair.

"Oh!" Lucy gasped. It echoed throughout the bathroom.

Shannon's wet hair was hanging on a small suction hook in the shower. It was a wig! And Shannon was right beside it—bald!

8

Keeping Secrets

Wednesday night . . .

She looked so . . . different. Lucy couldn't take her eyes off of Shannon's smooth head.

The water was immediately turned off, and Shannon cried through the curtain. "What are you doing in here? You're spying on me!"

"I wasn't spying!" Lucy said. "I . . . I promise. I just came back to get my mom's shampoo. I'll find it and . . . um, leave!" She began backing away, toward the other showers.

"No . . . wait," Shannon said. "I'll be out in a minute. Please don't leave before I come out."

Mrs. Rice came into the room and looked around. Lucy waved a quick hi. Mrs. Rice nodded and, not hearing any more commotion, left.

Lucy located her mom's shampoo bottle and sat down on one of the scratchy concrete benches in the dressing area. The night air in the room was clean and cool, but her brain was as foggy as the steam evaporating through the window and into the night. How could a girl be bald? And how come no one had noticed?

Just a few minutes later Shannon came out in her pj's. With her hair on. She sat down next to Lucy.

"I guess you know now," she said.

"I'm so sorry," Lucy said. "I didn't mean to find you. I'm really sorry."

"Really sorry you found me, or really sorry I'm bald?" Shannon asked.

Lucy sat there for a minute. "Both, I guess."

Shannon nodded. "Now you know why I don't tell anyone. They always feel sorry for me. Or think I'm a freak."

A question tumbled out of Lucy's mouth before she could stop it. "Have you always been bald?"

Shannon shook her head. "Not always. A few years ago I developed a condition called alopecia. First my hair started falling out in patches, and then it started staying bald in circles. Pretty soon it all fell out, and it never grew back." She wiggled her eyebrows. "I'm glad I kept my eyebrows, though. A lot of kids don't."

Lucy ran her hand over her own eyebrows and then over her hair. She'd never appreciated her hair like that before.

"I like to do that to my hair now, too," Shannon said.

"Why do you shower every night?" Lucy asked. "I'm sorry, that was rude."

"No. I take the wig off and put antibacterial lotion inside it every night, and I wash the oils off of my scalp.

"People treat me totally different when they know I'm bald," Shannon went on. "They make fun of me, don't look me in the eye. I look up and they're staring and pretending they're not. They ask a lot of questions." Shannon cheered up. "But that's all changed now since I got the wig." She shook her head. "Isn't it pretty?"

Lucy's heart slivered, both for the purity of Shannon's smile and the jealousy she'd felt toward Shannon for that lovely blond hair. "It is truly pretty," she answered softly. "Is there anything you can't do? Oh! I'm sorry, I'm asking more questions." *And feeling sorry for you, and trying not to stare at your scalp line and see where the wig starts. Which I'm not supposed to do.* Lucy kept her eyes down.

"Well," Shannon said softly, "I won't dive. I think that the force of diving might rip my wig off."

Lucy visualized the horrible possibility: Shannon dives into the water and the wig rips off and floats to the top of the pool. Shannon breaks the water surface, as she must, and everyone—including the boys—stares and points and gasps at her bald head.

Lucy shook her head to clear the image.

"What are you going to do about the competition?"

"Sit out." Shannon frowned. "I know the Wrens are going to be so mad. We're ahead tonight, you know. Winning. They're so excited to win the Golden Pig's Foot together."

"They won't be mad when you tell them why."

"I'm not telling them why."

"Why not?"

"I have spent *years* being the bald girl. The girl

everyone pitied and was friends with because people felt sorry for or because their moms or teachers or counselors told them to be nice to me and be glad they didn't have my problem. So now I have a wig! And no one knows. Jessica is just starting to be my real friend," Shannon smiled. "She's moving into your bunk tonight, you know. I'm a normal girl, Lucy, for one time in my life. Can you understand how that feels?"

Lucy nodded. "I guess so."

Shannon dragged her foot along the cool tile on the bathroom floor. "When you came to Catalina this summer, would you have told all those girls in your cabin the first week you knew them, 'Oh, by the way, I'm bald'? "

Lucy thought back to her first week. The other girls had seemed cool, not very friendly. She wasn't even sure at that point if Serena was going to keep the diary a secret, much less something so personal and scary as baldness. Even her second week, Lucy had wanted them to like her just for herself, which was why she hadn't let Serena deliver the party invitations with her.

"No," Lucy said. "You're right. I wouldn't have told them. No way. There are . . . there are some of them I probably wouldn't tell right now."

"So you know how I feel. I love feeling normal, Lucy. Wearing pretty hair clips, having people like me or not like me as they get to know me, and not labeling me as the 'poor little bald girl' first. I am who I am. I know that."

Shannon tucked her drying hair behind her ears. "And someday I might tell Jessica if we stay friends after camp. When I know we're friends for real. But I don't tell others.

That way I get to feel normal, Lucy. It's a blessing from God."

"Does Helen know?" Lucy asked. "I mean, she knows you come in here by yourself."

"No. My mom told me I didn't have to tell anyone, but she told Mrs. Rice." Shannon pointed at the director's wife, who was installing more paper towels into the holders in the next room. "Mrs. Rice said she'd stay in here every night when I shower. She just told Helen that my mom asked that I shower alone." Shannon smiled. "Helen thinks I'm modest. One day she told me that she was just like me—she was very modest, too. Isn't that cool? She doesn't think she has to protect or baby me. She just thinks we're alike!"

Shannon's face beamed, and then she stood up. "We'd better get back to our cabins. Promise you'll keep my secret?"

"I promise."

Lucy headed back to Squirrel. Rachel, looking worried, met her at the door.

"Lucy! I was just coming to find you. I didn't realize you were gone. Please don't do that again—remember the buddy system."

In a daze, Lucy agreed. They all got in bed early— tomorrow morning was the sacrifice walk and they would all get up before dawn and get dressed without saying a word.

"It's a sacrifice of silence," Rachel said of the silent walk to the top of the mountain behind camp to watch the sun rise. "We're giving up the right to talk to anyone until lunchtime, speaking only to God, in our hearts. In the silence, maybe we can hear Him more clearly."

Lucy crawled under her covers, and then the lights went out. *I'm sorry, Jesus,* she spoke in her heart. *I was so jealous. I guess you just never know about anyone else, do you? I need to love others as best I can, no matter what. Please forgive me. And please let Shannon have a fantastically normal week. She deserves it.*

The cool wind blew through the screen, and soon enough Lucy was snuggling into sleep.

Her last thoughts before slipping into a dream were, *I have to make sure that I am extra careful with what I say so that I keep Shannon's secret. And I hope she can keep it all week, too.*

Sacrifice of Silence

Thursday morning . . . D Day minus one

They straggled up the hill Thursday morning, single file, girl and boy campers and counselors. Lucy hadn't tied her shoes, and the laces flopped on the sides like snake tongues with every step till she laced them up. Who would have thought laces could sound so loud in the silence? Almost everyone carried something for the cowboy breakfast—a pot, a pan, garbage bags, or paper plates. Lucy carried one of the plastic coolers with bacon in it.

The climb was rocky, and sometimes small rocks broke loose and tumbled down the side. The trail wound around, too. The Wren girls walked ahead of the Squirrel girls. Lucy watched Shannon for a while. Shannon couldn't see Lucy, so it wasn't staring, was it?

At least if I have to be silent, I can't accidentally blurt out anything suspicious.

The birds were out and the wind blew, but no one

spoke. The day was peaceful and newborn. Lucy kept her mind on God, His creation around her, and His power. She glanced at Shannon again.

What would it be like to be bald? What if no one ever waited to see what was in your heart before judging you? What if camp were ruined for Shannon?

When they got to the top, the sun began to spread across the crust of the horizon. Each camper dumped his or her contribution by the eating place and then took a card with a Bible verse on it. They scattered along the cliff top, meditating on the verse on their card.

Lucy's card read, *Live a life filled with love for others, following the example of Christ, who loved you and gave himself as a sacrifice to take away your sins. And God was pleased, because that sacrifice was like a sweet perfume to him. Ephesians 5:2.*

Serena sat just a few feet from Lucy, and the others were speckled across the rounded hilltop like candy sprinkles. But somehow Lucy felt completely alone with God. After watching the sky pinken a bit, Lucy looked at her verse again and smiled.

I remember when I got my first perfume, Lord. It was Love's Baby Soft, and it came in a pretty pink bottle. It smelled more grown-up than baby powder but not as strong as her mom's Chanel No. 5. Lucy had sprayed it all over herself and then run through the house. Her dad said that cats had bells on their collars so owners could keep track of them, but they didn't need a bell to know where Lucy was. All they had to do was sniff.

Lucy giggled. She loved that sweet scent. She moved

her legs from beneath her, and a few rocks dribbled away.

The counselors began fixing breakfast, and soon the perfume of bacon scented the clean coastal air. Lucy stared out over the water. The sunlight caught each wave for just a second; it looked like hundreds of camera flashes snapping over the water.

Once breakfast was ready, they sat together. No one spoke, but everyone smiled. Lucy even felt close to the Hunky Monkeys today. Lucy stared over at Shannon, whose hair was not done up in clips or curls or ribbons today. It hung loose and untidy around her shoulders like the other girls wore theirs. A normal girl among normal girls.

Afterward, Lucy sat on a big rock with her verse card. *Sacrifice*. What did that really mean?

Lucy closed her eyes and remembered last spring's softball season. It was a tight game—they were the home team, it was the bottom of the last inning, and they were tied. Lucy was waiting on third, but there was one out already. The girl who came up to bat was not, as they say, a power hitter.

While Lucy and the third-base coach watched in amazement, the girl hit the ball right along the first-base line and ran toward it. By the time she got there, she was tagged out.

But during that time Lucy ran like her feet were on fire and had made it safely home. Her point counted, and her run won it for their team. But the real hero was the girl who had hit a sacrifice to first base. She got herself out on purpose so that the team could win. The whole team knew it. The hitter was a hero.

Did you hit a sacrifice for us, Jesus? Bring us safely home? Lucy said in her heart. Tears filled her eyes.

"Thank you," she whispered.

They trekked back down and later ate lunch together. The laughter was louder and the talk more exciting because of the silence that had come before. They were closer together.

"You know what today is?" Serena smiled.

"No. What?"

"The art competition."

"Well," Lucy teased, "since we have an award-winning artist with us here today, we know who will do well in that!"

Serena grinned. "Come on, it's our turn!" The girls trooped over to the art hut. The Wrens had just left. Their projects were still on the tables. There were three cute paintings, one weird sculpture, and four pretty good ones.

"I guess I'll do papier-mâché. I can't goof that up too bad." Lucy sat down next to Serena as Serena hummed and smiled and sketched out a scene of the two of them sitting on the skinned log by the beach.

Lucy's papier-mâché kept slumping. And the mouth of her vase kept folding in, so no flowers in it would be able to stick up. When their time was almost up, Lucy was in despair.

Julie stepped over and looked at Lucy's project on her way to hand in her own painting. "What is that?" She pointed at Lucy's project. "A beehive?"

Lucy looked at her piece. It did look like a beehive. Especially if she left it gray, which meant she wouldn't have to paint it. Lucy hated painting. *Yeah. A beehive. Great idea.*

"As a matter of fact, it is," Lucy said. She smiled and followed Julie to the table to turn in her piece.

The counselor in charge of art looked startled when Lucy handed over her gray mound.

"It's a beehive," Lucy explained.

The counselor smiled. "Oh. It's not too artsy, but . . . it's clever."

At least I didn't blow it, Lucy thought.

After the Alien Dinner with peeled grape eyeballs and spaghetti noodle tentacles prepared by the Hunky Monkeys and the Winning Warthogs, they all went to the beach for a marshmallow roast.

Lucy and Serena sat down near the water, by a small fire. The boys brought the roasting stuff by, and Lucy and Serena each skewered a sweet white pillow on a stick.

"I like mine good and burned," Lucy said.

"Not me. Lightly toasted," Serena responded.

Lucy ate marshmallows until she felt like her stomach was going to pop. Soon Shannon came and sat down on the other side of Lucy.

"Hi!" Lucy said. *I will not stare at her wig,* she reminded herself. *I won't.*

They chatted for a while and then grew silent. Serena kicked her shoes off and went to watch the others play volleyball.

Lucy glanced at Shannon out of the corner of her eye. "What's the matter?"

"I have to tell them tomorrow about diving," Shannon said. "I hope they're not mad. They're hoping to win." She smiled. "Okay, so I'll have one really bad day at camp. But all the others were terrific. It's so great to be treated like everyone else."

"But—" Lucy started.

Just then Jessica called, "Shannon! We need another person for volleyball!"

The grin that lit Shannon's face was as bright as the full moon smiling. "Coming!"

She nodded good-bye to Lucy and ran off. As she watched Shannon play volleyball, Lucy knew one thing for sure. Shannon was getting her wish to be normal. Everyone was treating her just like everyone else. No one knew her secret. Lucy would keep that secret, too.

Lucy saw one of the boys' counselors standing by the lifeguard chair. He was the same counselor in charge of swimming the other day and had watched the belly-flop fest. Lucy knew he'd be in charge of diving, too.

The sand flew behind her as Lucy raced over to the counselor. She looked around. No one else was nearby.

"Excuse me," she began.

"Yes?"

"I was just wondering," Lucy began, "what if someone didn't want to do the diving competition tomorrow? Like, if they couldn't really dive. Could they just sit out?"

"No," he said. "We don't want anyone to sit out. Of course, everyone can't be good at everything. The whole idea is that we all participate whether we're good or not. That's how a team works. Some people are good at art;

some are good at rope climbing. It's everyone working and cheering one another on that makes it teamwork, no matter what their abilities. We can't force anyone to participate, of course, but you'd get zero points for that event."

He looked straight at Lucy. "You don't have to be good, you know. You can always belly flop."

Lucy didn't get it for a minute, but he kept staring. Suddenly she realized, *Hey! He thinks it's me I'm talking about! And that I can't really dive because I'm bad at it. And that I want to sit out!*

"Thanks," she said abruptly and walked away. *The nerve of him. I may make beehive papier-mâché, but I can dive.*

When she got back to their spot, Serena had joined the volleyball game. Lucy didn't want to cut in midway through a game, so she sat in the sand and watched. Shannon was laughing out loud.

One last night of it, Lucy thought. *It's too bad that diving is the last day. The Wrens will think it's not fair, and they'll blame Shannon.*

She looked back at the counselor she had just talked to. *He thought I wanted to sit out.* A thought hit her.

What if I did sit out?

Lucy thought it over. If Lucy sat out, too, then the two winning teams would be evenly matched. They were way ahead of the other two girls' cabins, Lucy knew. Even Rachel had let something slip about that.

If Lucy sat out, the teams would be evened up. The Wrens might think it was fair, then, and not be mad at Shannon.

But if Lucy sat out, the Squirrels could lose. No one on her team would know *why* Lucy sat out. It would make no sense. She'd be seen as betraying Serena and all of the very friends who'd made her one of their own. They'd be mad.

If Lucy dove, the Squirrels would win for sure, because Shannon would have no points.

But if Lucy sat out, the Squirrels might lose. She could be responsible for their losing the last chance at the Golden Pig's Foot. And since they'd never understand why Lucy sat out, she'd probably lose most of her friends.

Lucy sighed. What was she going to do?

Dive

Friday morning . . . D Day!

On the way to breakfast that morning, all of the Squirrels noted with glee that they were on top of the stack. "Look! We're winning!" Amy pointed out.

"Now if we can just keep it that way through the rest of the day, we'll be carrying those little golden beauties home this week," Erica said.

They walked in, grabbed some oatmeal, and sat down. Lucy stared into her bowl. The raisins in the oatmeal looked like shriveled bug bodies. The brown sugar on top looked like sand. She pushed the bowl away and ate only the banana.

When she glanced over at the Wren table, she saw Shannon stand up quickly and leave the table. No one called to her to come back. They all sat in silence until she cleared the door, and then they began to whisper.

After breakfast they all went back to the room,

chattered, and then began to pack a few things and eventually put on their bathing suits. Lucy and Amy played a game of chess, and Lucy won even though she was totally distracted.

Finally Serena grabbed Lucy's hand. "Your diving day is here, my dear! Come on, let's go."

They strolled over to the pool, where the boys were finishing up. The boys sat in the bleachers on one side, while the girls sat down on the four metal benches behind the pool. Everyone was calling and cheering, whistling no matter who was up. The two losing teams went first. Some of them *did* belly flop, and a few actually held their bodies straight till they hit the bottom. Nobody, as far as Lucy could tell, touched the bull's-eye in the center of the pool or brought up one of the rings.

They wouldn't be winning, for sure. But they didn't seem to mind that much. Wrens and Squirrels, on the other hand, were all sitting on their hands, mouths closed, waiting.

The Wrens went first. The sting of chlorine started to burn Lucy's nose, and the sun was beginning to burn her skin. In her confusion that morning, she hadn't put any sunscreen on. The splash of the water, the sharp clapping . . . Normally it was pure fun for her. Not today.

One by one, the Wrens dove. They weren't great, but Lucy had to admit they were pretty good. It could be tough for the Squirrels to beat them. And when it came down to the sixth diver, Shannon, she stayed on the bench.

Helen went over and talked with her, giving her one last chance, Lucy assumed. Shannon gave a quick little no with a shake of her head. Helen smiled anyway and hugged her around the shoulder.

"All right!" Julie said. "We have it wrapped up now! That blond girl isn't going to dive! She'll get no points at all, and we're going to win."

Lucy felt dizzy. *Must be the chlorine.*

The two new Wrens each dove, and, Lucy thought, they dove well. After toweling off, they returned to the bench. No one looked at Shannon, and they sat far enough away that they wouldn't risk touching her.

Shannon kept her head down. Lucy felt sick. Shannon had been right. It was one bad day at camp for her so far.

Now it was time for the Squirrels.

Erica went first, and she dove a nice, clean dive. Amy went next and did all right. Lydia followed suit, and then Kelly, who actually got a ring. Betsy and Julie followed. Lucy tallied the moves. If Serena held her own, they'd be nearly equal after Serena's dive.

She should have been cheering on Serena. Instead, Lucy closed her eyes.

She wanted to win so badly. She wanted to help win, to do something good, like everyone else did. She'd wanted that all week. Yesterday's memory verse sat in the pocket of her cover-up.

God, this kind of sacrifice is not like the softball kind. That time, the batter sacrificed for our team. I want to be a good contributor to the team.

A thought occurred. Who was the team—the real team? Was it the Squirrels? Or was it . . . all of them?

I don't want to sit out, Lord. I really don't. No one will know I can dive. They'll think I chickened out instead. In that softball game, everyone knew she was doing it for all of us. This time, no one will know why I'm sacrificing. . . .

Lucy felt her metal Wired for Christ necklace warm up in the sun, burning her neck a little. She touched her fingers to it.

Shannon will know. Christ will know.

Serena came back to the bench. "Your turn! Finally!" she whispered.

Lucy willed her legs to stay on the bench. And suddenly it wasn't so hard to stay seated. Tears welled up in her eyes and she blinked them away. The Squirrels might be mad. They might lose. But no matter what the results, this was the right thing for her to do.

"I'm sitting out," Lucy said quietly.

"Stop joking, Lucy," Julie said. "Come on."

"Go, Lucy! Come on, it's your turn!" Serena urged.

Rachel came over to her and Lucy explained, "I feel like I should sit out. It . . . it makes it more fair to have seven from each team, since Shannon sat out."

"You don't have to do this, you know," Rachel said.

"I know," Lucy said. "I choose to."

Rachel indicated to the judge that they were done, and everyone began to scatter from the pool.

Lucy watched the Wrens. They weren't ignoring Shannon now. As they passed by, Lucy saw one of them pat Shannon's shoulder and say, "Well, don't worry about it now. One of them sat out, too, so things are still fair and square."

Lucy sighed. It looked a lot friendlier there than it felt

here. The Squirrels stood up. No Squirrel looked Lucy in the eye except Julie. "You really can't dive, can you? You were lying to us all along."

"I can dive. I just wanted things to be fair for the Wrens. Seven of them dove, seven of us dove."

"She had her chance. She chose to sit out. You didn't have to make things fair," Erica said, more with confusion than with meanness. "She chose to make it unfair for her team."

"Let's go get lunch. That sorry award is gone," Julie said. The others followed. Amy and Serena both looked at Lucy. They looked confused, but at least not mad. Serena followed them. "I'll be right back," she told Lucy.

Lucy waited till they had all been in the lunchroom for a long time and then went in and took a wrapped sandwich. She brought it outside and sat on a bench by herself.

She unwrapped the plastic wrap and took a bite. The ham slipped out from between the slices of bread and landed at her feet.

A tear slipped out. She picked up the piece of ham and threw the whole sandwich in the trash. She stared at her hands, looking at the now-chipped nail polish she'd painted on with her mom.

I wish you were here, Mom.

Lucy sighed and took yesterday's verse card out of the pocket of her cover-up. She unfolded it twice and smoothed out the creases. *Live a life filled with love for others, following the example of Christ, who loved you and gave himself as a sacrifice to take away your sins. And God was pleased, because that sacrifice was like sweet perfume to him.*

My sacrifice smells like chlorine to me, Lord. It makes my eyes cry.

Serena came back out of the lunchroom. She sat down next to Lucy.

"So what happened?" she finally asked. "Why did you change your mind?"

Lucy looked at her. "I didn't change my mind. I had a change of heart."

Serena stared.

"I just wanted things to be fair for the Wrens, too. For things to be equal."

"Shannon made that decision, Lucy. She made things unequal. It's not up to you to fix it. Congratulating her about the bunny and all is fine, but isn't this going too far?"

"Everybody's mad at me, right?"

"Julie is. The others are just . . . confused. They like you. But they also wanted to win and thought you did, too."

Lucy nodded. "I do."

"I know." Serena looked right at Lucy. "I don't know if we'll win or not. But you're still my best friend."

Shannon came out of the lunchroom and saw Lucy and Serena. Lucy met her gaze.

Shannon broke off with the others and came over to Lucy. "Thanks. Are you okay?"

Lucy was afraid the tears would spill again, so she just nodded.

Shannon sat down next to her. She looked at Serena. "Are you her best friend?"

Serena nodded.

Shannon was quiet for a moment and then stood up. "Would you both please come with me?"

Unexpected Deeds

Friday afternoon . . .

Shannon silently led them to Wren. When she opened the door, there were girls in the cabin. So they left and went to the bathroom. "This is the only place we can be alone," Shannon said. "I've got something to tell you."

Serena really looked puzzled now.

"You don't have to say anything," Lucy said. "I know you don't want to."

"I know," Shannon said. "It's my choice." Her face darkened. "Just this one person."

They sat down on one of the concrete benches. "What are we doing?" Serena asked.

Shannon turned to Lucy. "I guess it's kind of neat that we talk about this here, since this is where it all started." She turned toward Serena. "Can you keep a secret? I mean, really keep it?"

Serena looked more and more puzzled. "Yes."

Shannon slowly slid her pinky under her wig, lifting a piece of it up just a bit so Serena could see that it was, indeed, a wig.

"Oh!" Serena gasped.

"Uh-huh," Shannon said.

Lucy watched as Serena looked at Shannon with new eyes—pitying her, Lucy could see. Shannon had been right. It was how people reacted. She could see now why Shannon wanted to avoid that.

"Now you know why I wouldn't dive," Shannon said, whispering so that her words wouldn't echo through the lonely bathroom. "I was afraid my wig might come off. And I can't wear a diving cap. It can rip the hair out, and I'm afraid the tightness of the cap might pull the wig off."

"Your hair . . ." Serena started to say something.

"It's a wig. I have a condition called alopecia, and it makes all of your hair fall out. Most of us stay bald for a long time—just wearing hats and scarves or nothing, and getting pointed at. But now, some kids who have long hair cut theirs and donate the hair to wigmakers. It takes several kids' hair to make one wig for someone like me."

"Wow. I didn't know that," Lucy said. So someone had cut off her own beautiful hair to give it to someone like Shannon.

"Their hair will grow back, but kids like me will never have hair any other way. It took us a long time to afford this wig."

Serena squeezed Lucy's hand. "I'm sorry I was kind of mad at you. I should have known you had a good reason to sit out."

"Why are you telling Serena?" Lucy asked. "I thought you didn't want anyone to know."

"I don't," said Shannon. "And I don't plan on telling anyone else. Not even Jessica—yet. Maybe later. We've exchanged addresses for after camp." She smiled. "I told Serena because you did something very hard for me, and I wanted to do something to pay you back, so that at least one person would understand you. I didn't want it to hurt *your* friendship."

"Thanks," Lucy said.

"Thank *you*," Shannon said.

Serena turned to Lucy. "I really just wanted us to win so we could all have the award together, the team. I wanted everyone to know how great you are, like I do."

"I know," Lucy said. "But I guess I was learning who the real team was. All of us, you know. Christians." She thought about the other Squirrels and about her own experience at another camp many years ago. "And those who are watching us."

An announcement came over the loudspeaker.

"Campers! Please report to the archery field for the final competition of the week!"

Shannon said good-bye and left.

Well, Lucy thought, *we haven't lost yet.* She hadn't had a chance to read the archery paper again. She hoped she remembered it all.

Lucy and Serena scampered over to the archery field, still in bathing suits and cover-ups. The rest of the girls had already changed to shorts.

Serena took the seventh place in line, and Lucy took

the eighth. Amy turned and offered a small smile to Lucy.

Thank you, Amy.

The Squirrels went first this time, since they'd gone last for diving. Each of the first six got pretty close, except for Erica, who never hit inside the target. Serena went next—and got in the outside ring. Each girl got three shots.

Then it was Lucy's turn.

"I hope she doesn't sit out," Julie whispered. No one responded.

Lucy pulled the bow back once and let the arrow fly. It landed on the ground, next to Erica's stray shot.

The second shot hit inside the second line.

"Way to go!" Serena shouted. Lucy looked over at her. Serena seemed more determined than ever to cheer Lucy on. Lucy looked at the bull's-eye again and remembered her paper.

There was no wind to adjust for. The last shot had hit a little high and left, so Lucy sighted down an inch lower and to the right.

She let go, the line snapped, and the arrow hit just inside the bull's-eye.

"Hooray!" The Squirrels jumped up and came over to her. "Great shot!"

Lucy felt warm and the sting from the chlorine left her eyes. By the time she and her teammates looked up, though, half the Wrens had shot.

"Did any of the Wrens hit a bull's-eye?" Julie asked Rachel. "We weren't paying attention."

"I'm not sure. I wasn't watching," she said. "I heard a big cheer go up for them, though."

The Squirrels quieted down. "Oh. Uh-oh."

Lucy's shot might not mean so much after all. The next four Wrens shot well, as well as the Squirrels had, but no bull's-eye. It all depended on what those first four had done. No one knew for sure.

The awards ceremony was coming up. In just a few hours, all would be known.

Because the other girls had already changed, Lucy and Serena raced back to their cabin to change. When Lucy opened her drawer, she saw the box of hair color.

"The Diary Deed!" she said. "We have to do it today!"

"Um . . ." Serena sat down on her bed, twirling her hair. "I guess it's not such a big deal to color it, when you consider that we at least *have* hair. It's cool of those other girls to donate some of theirs."

"Yeah." Lucy stood up and looked Serena in the eye. "I wonder how much hair you need to have in order to donate some."

"Not so much, I bet. Since a lot of kids' hairs are put together to make the wig."

Lucy took a deep breath. "Are you thinking what I'm thinking?"

Serena stopped twirling her hair. "I think so."

The girls quickly changed into their good clothes and then raced over to Wren to get Shannon. Lucy explained what they were going to do, and Shannon hugged them both. "That is so cool. But do we have to tell Wendy why?"

"No," Lucy promised. "We already told her we wanted to do our hair special for the ceremony."

"Okay. But you know you'll have to cut it to at least

your shoulders in order to donate enough." Shannon got a plastic bag from her suitcase and brought it with them to put the hair into. "My mom packed extras for dirty clothes," she said, giggling.

They ran to Wendy's cabin. After knocking on the door, they finally heard Wendy answer. "Hey, you two!"

"Wendy," Lucy said, "can you please help us?"

She quickly asked Wendy to cut their hair for the ceremony. Wendy giggled. "All right, if you're sure. You two call your mothers." She tossed them her cell phone.

Serena went into the bathroom so Wendy wouldn't hear her and dialed her mother. Lucy didn't want to breathe down Serena's back while she talked, so she stared out the window instead. Would this work? Would it look kooky? Would it all turn out okay?

She imagined them walking into the awards ceremony and closed her eyes.

Serena came back and handed the phone to Lucy. "I got the go-ahead. It's your turn."

Lucy went into the bathroom and called her mother. Thankfully, Mom was still home. They were just about to leave to come to the awards ceremony. Lucy talked with her for a few minutes and then came out of the bathroom. "She said okay."

Lucy went first. Wendy brought out her comb and scissors. She misted Lucy's hair and began to cut—not too short, but just exactly where Lucy showed her to cut. Lucy raised her eyes at Shannon, who nodded.

"I guess this is the closest we'll ever come to doing exactly what the diary girls did as a deed." Lucy tried to lighten the conversation, but all the while she was thinking, *I hope I don't look like a geek.*

"You're right!" Serena said. She looked at Lucy. "Don't worry. It looks great."

When Wendy was done, she wrapped a ponytail holder around the hair she'd cut off and handed it to Lucy.

Lucy, in turn, handed it to Shannon. Wendy looked at them funny but didn't ask questions.

Shannon slipped two of her jeweled clips out of her hair and slipped them into Lucy's. Lucy turned to face the mirror, holding her breath.

It looked . . . cute! Not too short—it still reached her shoulders. She could still pull it back a little and could make some tiny braids. Lucy's head felt light, and her back felt exposed where the hair used to lie.

"I'm next," Serena said. Wendy misted her hair, too, and began to clip. The scissors sounded like the trimmer Lucy's dad used at home to edge the lawn. Serena's hair, too, was bundled, and she handed it to Shannon.

"I collect them," Shannon said.

"Okay, whatever." Wendy smiled, and the three girls began to laugh.

Shannon took her last two clips out and placed them in Serena's hair. "Now you two will match at the awards assembly tonight."

"You look absolutely adorable," Lucy told Serena. "Like a beautiful doll."

Serena fluffed her hair. "It's pretty, actually."

Unexpectedly, Shannon hopped up into Wendy's chair. "What are you doing?" Wendy asked.

"Will you please cut one small piece of my hair, about this long?" She indicated two inches with her fingers.

Wendy found a piece on the underside of Shannon's head and cut it. If she noticed it was a wig, she said nothing. And, in fact, the wig did look very real. Shannon hopped down from the chair and took a piece of Serena's hair and a piece of Lucy's hair from the bundle. She braided it into a tiny plait and tied it at both ends with rubber bands. Then she handed it to Lucy. "So you'll always remember how thankful I am," she whispered softly enough for only Lucy to hear.

Lucy swallowed. Her hair would grow back, and so would Serena's. That piece that Shannon cut out of her wonderful wig would never grow back, though. A silent sacrifice. Wendy stepped into the bathroom to get ready for the ceremony, and the girls were free to talk.

"I'll take this back home and send it in to the place that makes the wigs," Shannon said. "You both have great unique hair. It will be an awesome gift to combine your hair with some other kids' hair and make a wig for a girl like me."

She hugged them both, and Lucy and Serena hugged her back. Then they played around in front of the mirror for a while. Lucy clipped her hair back, thinking how it would look gelled or curled or braided. "Even if we don't like it, it will grow back."

"But I do like it," Serena said. "It's just another thing to bring us closer together. *And* we did our Diary Deed!"

Lucy smiled. "Let's stay in Wendy's cabin till the awards ceremony and make a surprise entrance."

"I'll go and tell Rachel," Shannon said.

"Lots of surprises," Serena said as Shannon left.

"Like who wins the Golden Pig's Foot." Lucy's stomach flipped as she said the words out loud.

The Award

Friday evening . . .

Lucy and Serena approached the dining room holding hands and giggling. The scoreboards outside had been taken down. Inside the room waited their parents, the rest of the campers, and the awards.

"Wow!" Erica called out first from their table. "Look at you guys! Awesome 'do!"

Lucy and Serena turned to one another and smiled. They hadn't been fooling themselves after all. It did look okay!

Their parents were waiting at the table with the other Squirrels and their parents, laughing and chatting together. Except for Julie. Julie's mom didn't talk to anyone, not even Julie.

"Luce!" Her mom ran up and hugged her. Lucy hugged her mom back, hard. Mom ran her hands through Lucy's hair and smiled. "It looks nice." Lucy hadn't realized until this minute how much she'd missed Mom. She held out her hands and showed her mom her nails.

"They're chipped from swimming, but they're still green," she said.

"Hey!" said Dad. "Don't I get a hug?" Lucy turned toward her father. "I missed you, Sparky." Dad's beard tickled, such a reassuring feeling.

"I think the haircut makes you look much more grown-up, Chiquita," Serena's mom said. "You too, Lucy-lu."

Lucy giggled. She looked around the table. No one was really ignoring her. But it wasn't peppy, either.

They all drank lemonade, the Larsons across the table from the Romeros, waiting for the program to begin. As they chatted, Lucy saw Serena's eyes open wide and look behind Lucy. Lucy turned around.

"Oh, hi, Jake!" she said.

He blushed and held his hands behind his back. "Hi. Your hair looks . . . uh, really nice," he said. Then he looked at Serena. "You too," he added politely.

Lucy could tell Serena was going to tease her, and she gave her a look across the table that said, "Please be quiet!"

"Anyway," Jake said, "I realized that last week I told you I was bringing some candy to camp. I forgot to share it with you Squirrels. Sorry. The boys gobbled it all up. Anyway," he added, "I called my dad and asked him to bring you guys something new from the shop. I thought these would be kind of appropriate." He handed over a plastic bag.

They were Jelly Bellies, all right, but they looked

different. Some of them were squashed, some were joined together.

"They're called Belly Flops," Jake said. "I thought of it because of, you know, your belly flop the other day."

No one mentioned diving. Lucy laughed and took the bag. "Thanks."

Jake walked away, and Lucy set jelly beans in the middle of the table for everyone to share.

Lucy looked over at Jessica and Shannon. "I'll be right back," she said, checking her watch. The program would start any minute.

She ran over to the Wren table and hugged Helen. "Thanks for making it easy for me this week," she said.

"No problem," Helen said. "You're a great girl."

The other Wrens said good-bye to Lucy, too, each of them hugging her. When Lucy hugged Shannon, she caught the distinct scent of Love's Baby Soft perfume. She giggled.

My sacrifice smells like perfume now.

As she left the table, Lucy noticed Jessica crowded up against Shannon, who was laughing with honest pleasure.

Lucy went back to her own table and waited. Her dad and Mr. Romero were involved in a lengthy discussion about deep-sea fishing, which they both loved. Serena was talking with Erica, and the moms chatted about the heat.

"Ladies and gentlemen, young ladies and young gentlemen," Mr. Rice began. Everyone quieted down, and the slideshow began. They all laughed when the rope-climb slides were shown, with the muddy Monkey. Everyone looked at Lucy when the belly-flop slides went up—she hadn't even known they were taking them!

Next they saw Shannon playing volleyball with the Wrens. Shannon glowed, and Lucy couldn't be sure, but she thought Shannon's dad looked a little teary eyed.

"And now," Mr. Rice said, "the Golden Pig's Foot awards! Boys first."

"What? I thought girls went first," Serena said.

"Shh," Amy quieted her.

In spite of the rope-climb drop, the Hunky Monkeys won. Lucy felt bad for Jake and Philip and all of the other Winning Warthogs.

"Don't worry," Serena said across the table. "They won last year."

Mr. Rice continued. "The ladies provided stiff competition this year. Many days, it was just a matter of a point or two as to who was in first place. In fact, it came right down to the line today, as it sometimes does. And, in fact, down to the last event, archery."

He cleared his throat. "But there were some good shots—and one great one—right at the end."

Serena leaned over and whispered, "That was you!"

"Shh!" Erica said. "He's announcing the winner!"

Mr. Rice continued. "So I am pleased to present this year's Golden Pig's Foot to the Squirrels!"

All of them stood up and screamed, running around the table and hugging one another.

They each ran up and took one of the trophies, and Julie took an extra one for Jenny. They'd won!

Afterward, in the cool of the evening, they packed their rooms and said good-bye. The last thing Lucy did was unhook her screen, carefully reach for the empty cocoon, and slip it into a plastic bag. It was a reminder of something she didn't want to forget. Then she put the plastic bag near Tender Teddy.

"I won't see you in church this week because I'll be here again," Rachel said. "See you soon, though!"

They all hugged. "Let's meet at the beach next week sometime or the week after," Amy said.

Even Julie joked over all the competitions, but no one mentioned diving. When Lydia brought up belly flops and diving, Erica quickly changed the subject.

They'll probably never understand.

Finally Lucy and Serena and their parents piled into the Suburban. Once they were on the road, Serena took out the diaries, old and new.

She opened the old diary and began to read. " 'Dear Diary,' " the blocky writing began. " 'We didn't cut our hair after all.' "

"Ah! The rats!" Serena snapped the diary shut. "And here we cut our hair!"

Lucy began to giggle, and soon the two of them busted up laughing.

"What's going on?" Mrs. Romero asked.

"Oh, nothing," Serena said. She opened the diary back up and handed it to Lucy, who read the curly writing.

"We decided that there are reasons to make a change and reasons not to. Fitting in with everyone else is not a reason to make a change. So we drew our long hair back into tails and wore it

proudly among all the chop heads. And we feel good about it. Now, speaking of tails, Serena has a plan for next week.

Lucy handed the diary back over.

"We're both used to riding nags, and Serena wants a horse with power. I've never ridden a big horse, but I'm willing to try. Ta-ta till then, Diary.

Faithful Friends,
mary and Serena."

"Horses, cool," Lucy said. She looked out her window, and so did Serena.

"Should we write in *our* diary?" Serena asked.

Lucy nodded. As Serena fumbled for a pen, Lucy tugged her arm. "Look!" They drove right past the Double C Ranch, the one owned by Mrs. Romero's friend.

Serena looked at Lucy. "Are you thinking what I'm thinking?"

Lucy nodded. "Horses. We're there next week."

Serena wrote in the diary first. She sketched two girls doing belly flops and drew arrows that said *Lucy* and *Serena* with the word *Yowch!* next to it. She wrote about her silent morning verse, and how good it was to be bunkmates and how being apart for a few days had made them realize how much they liked being together.

Lucy wrote about their haircuts and Shannon. Then she neatly copied the verse from her sacrifice walk card.

There are good reasons to make a change, she wrote. *Changes from the inside out.*

As they closed the diary, they put in the three-strand braid of hair: blond, brown, and reddish-yellow. *Our team,* Lucy wrote, *and our braid.*

> *Faithful Friends,*
> *Lucy and Serena*

Just then, the car ran over a bump and squashed them together.

"That proves it." Serena giggled. "We're as close as two friends can be."

Do not change yourselves to be like
the people of this world.
But be changed within
by a new way of thinking.
Then you will be able to decide
what God wants for you.
And you will be able to know
what is good and pleasing to God
and what is perfect.

ROMANS 12:2 (ICB)

SANDRA BYRD and her best friend went to Girl Scout camp in fifth grade—and a mouse snuck into the sleeping bag of one of her cabinmates!

Sandra lives near beautiful Seattle, between snow-capped Mount Rainier and the Space Needle, with her husband and two children (and let's not forget her new puppy, Duchess). When she's not writing, she's usually reading, but she also likes to scrapbook, listen to music, and spend time with friends. Besides writing THE HIDDEN DIARY books, she's also the author of the bestselling series SECRET SISTERS.

For more information on THE HIDDEN DIARY series, visit Sandra's Web site: *www.sandrabyrd.com*. Or you can write to Sandra at

Sandra Byrd
P.O. Box 1207
Maple Valley, WA 98038

**Don't miss book seven
of THE HIDDEN DIARY,
Take a Chance!**

For a preview of Lucy and Serena's next diary adventure, just hold up this page in front of a mirror.

The diary girls ride stallions—big, bold, difficult horses—so Lucy wants to ride one, too. When she and Serena try to help save the Double C Ranch, though, that desire has to be put aside—for a few days. Lucy finds a hidden opportunity and climbs on a stallion anyway. She can't imagine the consequences of that one impulsive act—both for her and for the Double C.